Praise for *Secrets of the Plumed Saint*

It's rare when a book catches my interest by the end of the first sentence. But this is exactly what happened when I picked up Elizabeth Ann Galligan's manuscript, *Secrets of the Plumed Saint.* The spiritual and historical elements, which she magically wove into this tapestry of many colors, have illuminated my heart and elevated my spirit. At one point I found myself putting the book down, thinking I'd take a wee break, but immediately picked it right back up in order to digest more delicious, suspenseful details. I highly implore people of different faiths to read this book. Assuredly they will be enchanted by the many "secret" scents of New Mexico. The story, the artistic flow of words and scenes, the suspense – all expertly relayed by the poetic soul of Elizabeth Ann Galligan – offer to the readers an intriguing invitation to take a pilgrimage to the Land of Enchantment with its glorious traditions, customs and diverse cultures. Enjoy! And spread the word about the Little Child of New Mexico.

Daniel T. Paulos is Director of the Saint Bernadette Institute of Sacred Art and author of *Peace in the Midst of Chaos, Behold the Women,* and *He's Put the Whole World in Her Hands.*

Add this book to your library. While reading *Secrets of the Plumed Saint,* you will become immersed in the daily life of a rural village in northern New Mexico. Elizabeth Ann Galligan's characters have all the flaws and foibles of your neighbors, friends and family. Her description of the santero, Old Mister Benavídez, and the process he went through in creating the Plumed Saint (the Santo Nino de Atocha) is extremely interesting and reveals techniques used by traditional New Mexican saint carvers.

Gene Bundy is Special Collections librarian at Golden Library, Eastern New Mexico University, Portales, New Mexico.

The story of devotion to the Santo Niño de Atocha among the Hispano and Pueblo peoples in New Mexico is profound, and so is this story, *Secrets of the Plumed Saint.*

Sit down at your kitchen table and have a cup of coffee with these people. They are my family and friends, and their dilemma is at hand! They have secrets to discover and secrets to keep from the Church.

Elizabeth Ann Galligan has carefully crafted an intriguing story of a New Mexican village as it struggles to come to grips with the disappearance of its 100-year old image of the plumed saint. This is truly a New Mexican story, echoing the reality of the continued disappearance of *santos* from village chapels and Penitente *moradas.* I close my eyes and I recognize every one of the characters who live in Villa Vieja as they try to discover who stole the statue and why. At times, I wanted to jump into the story and help solve the mystery.

As a small child, I recall going to the shrine of the Santo Niño in Zuni Pueblo with my parents, Tía Lala, and my Nana Ignacia, where they presented the image of the Santo Niño de Atocha with new shoes. Their expectation was that he would don these shoes and, by night, travel far distances to perform miracles – and he did. In the 1980s as young parents, my wife, Debbie, and I took new shoes to the Santo Niño de Atocha at the famous Santuario in Chimayó, New Mexico, petitioning the same of the miraculous Holy Child just as my grandma had done a quarter century earlier.

Charles M. Carillo, Ph.D. is a saint carver and an expert on religious folk art of New Mexico. He is the subject of *Charlie Carillo: Tradition & Soul* and author of numerous publications. With Thomas J. Steele, S.J., he wrote *A Century of Retablos: The Janis and Dennis Lyon Collection of New Mexican Santos, 1780-1880.* Among other titles, he is the author of *Saints of the Pueblos* and *A Tapestry of Kinship.* He illustrated Peggy Pond Church's children's story, *Shoes for the Santo Niño.*

Secrets

of the

Plumed Saint

A Tale of Intrigue from Northern New Mexico

By

Elizabeth Ann Galligan

CREDITS

Dan Paulos: Cover design

The Armijo Family: In whose collection the Santo Niño rests

Charles Ortiz: Photographer and Spanish consultant

Melinda Beavers: Map Illustration of Villa Vieja

Peggy Herrington: Layout and design adviser

First Edition: 2012

ABQ PRESS TRADE PAPERBACK EDITION 2012

www.abqpress.com

ABQ Press
Albuquerque, New Mexico

ISBN 978-0-9838712-2-4

Dedication

To my parents,
Gerald Gregory Galligan & Elizabeth Eberhart Galligan,
who passed on their love of the land and the people
of northern New Mexico
to their children,
I return the gift.

To the Reader

Welcome to *Secrets of the Plumed Saint*. This is a work of fiction, a crime novel, set in northern New Mexico in the 1970s. When someone steals a 100-year old statue of the Santo Niño de Atocha bequeathed to the people of Villa Vieja, the villagers resolve to keep the news secret from the arrogant new priest and the Church hierarchy. Led by sleuths Jay Sierra and Ernie Lucero, the plot's twists and turns challenge the community to bring all of its talents, knowledge, and various allies to solve the mystery.

Events in the plot are fictional but plausible. During my research for the book, respondents shared their stories based on first-hand knowledge or remembrances passed down by families. In that sense, kernels of truth are scattered throughout. The author has enhanced the details and created the rest from her imagination.

But are the characters real? They are fictitious, created from an amalgam of traits melded together by the author. In each one, the reader will recognize common human foibles and strengths. They do not depict any actual person, living or dead, except for the mention of El Hermitaño. The hermit, a healer and holy man, known by various names, Juan María Justiniani and Giovanni María D'Agostini (other variations appear in the literature), actually lived on Cerro de Tecolote (Pilgrim's Peak) from 1863-1867. He wandered to southern New Mexico and lived in a cave near the foothills of the Organ Mountains. In 1869, the revered man was murdered. Who killed him is still a mystery.

The author has striven for accuracy and relied on a number of sources, human and written, for background information on rural Hispanic customs, saint-carving, Catholic religious practices, devotion to the Santo Niño de Atocha, and societal changes in the 1970s that

i

affected life in rural New Mexican areas. The author is responsible for any errors. The interested reader is referred to Juan Javier Pescador's book, *Crossing Borders with the Santo Niño de Atocha, 2009, UNM Press.*

Devotion to the lives of the saints and images of God in New Mexico resulted in distinctive forms. Images carved or painted on flat surfaces are called *retablos.* Three-dimensional carvings are *bultos.* The term *santo* may be somewhat confusing. The term *santo* as an adjective means "holy." As a noun, it refers to a carved image of a saint or is used to refer to a person, as in "She's a saint." In Roman Catholic theology, Christ is not a saint, but the Son of God. In the vernacular in the story, various names, such as The Holy Child, El Niño, The Christ Child, El Niñito, and the wandering saint, all refer to Jesus Christ or His image. "Santo Niño" means Holy Child, not Saint Niño.

Forms of worship and prayers in the small villages were woven into the fabric of their daily lives and passed on to the next generation. The people safeguarded their faith through long periods during which priests might visit once or twice a year. The people sustained their faith, and it sustained them. The devotion to the Virgin of Atocha and the Holy Child was carried to the Americas by the Spaniards. In 1704, a Castilian landowner commissioned a shrine near Fresnillo, Mexico, in which a statue of the Virgin of Atocha and the Holy Child was displayed. The people developed a special and separate devotion to the Holy Child. Over time, He was transformed from a newborn royal prince to a young man dressed as a pilgrim who ventured out at night to bring food, water and comfort to families in need. The Santo Niño de Atocha became the patron saint of the disabled, prisoners, travelers, prostitutes, mothers, anyone in desperate need, captives, and even thieves. From Old Mexico the devotion was introduced to New Mexico in the early 1800s.

Even in the 21st century, people attribute many miracles to the Santo Nino's continuing care and power to answer prayers. The image of the Santo Niño de Atocha presents a medieval pilgrim seated in a chair, holding a staff hung with water gourds in one hand and a basket of bread in the other. His most distinctive feature is a wide-brimmed hat decorated with a flourish of feathers – thus, "the plumed saint."

Acknowledgements

Writing a novel is not only an individual effort but a collaborative process guided by friends, allies, and unseen spirits. I owe a tremendous debt of gratitude to those who inspired me, held my hand, provided support and expertise and shouted encouragement. I laud the many generous people who helped along the way. If I have left out anyone, I apologize. Please know that your contributions also spurred me on.

Starting Line-up

At the center of the *Secrets of the Plumed Saint* is the disappearance of a 100-year-old wood carving of the Santo Niño de Atocha. When I asked Dr. Charles M. Carrillo, saint carver, professor historian, and well-known expert on religious folk art of the Southwest to act as consultant, he generously agreed. I cannot overstate the importance of his guidance in directing me to resources, both literary and human. Some anecdotes and stories he shared enliven the text. I am deeply grateful for the gift of his time and his support.

The next pillar of support I wish to thank is Dan Paulos, Director of the Saint Bernadette Institute of Sacred Art, Albuquerque, author and artist. From the first day, he encouraged me to continue on. He offered his own expertise and the gift of his time. His enthusiasm for the project sustained my writing from beginning to completion. No matter how busy, his comments on the text were meaningful and gracious. The results of his talent for artistic design are seen in the cover.

To Ernie R. Lujan, former Santa Fe police officer turned saint carver, I thank for his generosity in sharing his first-hand knowledge of art theft, police procedure, and techniques of saint carving, an unusual combination of expertise. His influences are found throughout the text and in the character of Ernie the cop. His comments about community solidarity gave me ideas for the ending.

To Mark David Gerson, author, writing teacher and guide, I extend my sincere gratitude. His patient counsel in his workshops and presentations encouraged me to listen always to the voice of the muse and to believe in my characters' voices. I learned about the spiritual component of the writing process from him. Without his guidance; the secrets of the plumed saint might not have been told.

Clerics

I thank the following men of the cloth who considered my ideas, gave suggestions and information, asked important questions, and offered a Christian perspective: the Reverend Father Thomas J. Steele, Society of Jesus; (dec.); the Reverend Father Patrick Valdez, pastor, San Luis, CO; the Reverend Father Casimiro Roca, Sons of the Holy Family and long-time pastor of El Santuario de Chimayó, Chimayó, NM; and the Rev. Father Paul A. Patitsas, Economos, former pastor of St. George Greek Orthodox Church, Albuquerque, whose parish was victimized by theft of its most sacred objects.

First Readers and Early Responders

I benefitted from the support and encouragement of friends, family and early supporters: Lucia Zimmitti, Judith Van Gieson, Patricio T. Trujillo, Cathrene Connery Daniel Acheson-Brown Elizabeth Self, Gene Bundy, Geni Flores, Mary Louise Sena, Diane Pinkey, Jeanie Hughes, Richard Hughes, Joyce Casey, Dorothea Fulton Frantz (dec.), Sara Frantz, Nora F. Booth, Dolly Flynn-Anaya, Suzanne G. Peet, Ruth Peet, Josie Sena, Luella Lopez, Felix Salazar, María Paulson, Ken Wells, my dear cousins, Eloise E. Chevrier, the Rev. David Chevrier, Dikkon Eberhart, and Gretchen E. Cherington; finally, to Arturo Sierra (dec.) who knew his surname would be used for the protagonist.

Special Thanks

For the friends and writers who read the entire manuscript, flaws and all: Charles M. Carrillo, Dan Paulos, Judith Van Gieson, Joyce Casey, Charles Ortiz, Renneé Durán, Suzanne Galligan Peet, Peggy Herrington, Dal Graham, María Garcia de Graham and Gene Bundy. Their gifts and questions improved the text.

The Supporting Cast

More thanks go to: Ron Sklar, Marina Morgan, Judith Pinson Berry, Stewart S. Warren, Mizaba D. Abedi, Liza E. Martinez, Ken Merrick, Joanne Bodin, Miguel Angel Acosta, David Bachelor, Luisa Duran,

José Barredo, James O'Lara, Muse Fan Club members Nancy La Turner; Victoria Daigneau and Ellen LaPenna; Peggy Herrington, Kay Snowfleet, Glenn Nicol, James B. Anderson, John J. Cordova Jr., John J. Candelaria, and for general support from my family, Gregory P. Scheib, Elizabeth H. Scheib, Irma S. Scheib, Geoffrey P. Scheib, Mia E. Maes, Reza Mirmesdagh, Suzanne Galligan Peet, Charles Peet, Patrick G. Galligan, Mary Hilbert, and Gerald P. Galligan.

Technical Help and Editorial Assistance
For the talents of Peggy Herrington, writing coach, for major editorial help and much more; Stewart S. Warren for IT assistance, Joyce Casey for editing and commentary, Rose Kern and Victoria Daigneau whose intervention saved the manuscript from vanishing into cyberspace, and, of course, to my publisher, ABQ Press, and Judith Van Gieson, for believing in the book.

Organizations and Conferences
I dared to think I could write a novel because of the stimulation of the *Tony Hillerman Mystery Writers Conferences*; 2006-2010, organized by Anne Hillerman and Jean Schaumberg. The conferences provided a wealth of writing tips, insights on craft and publishing, access to wonderful presenters, and networking opportunities with both accomplished and beginning writers.

To *SouthWest Writers,* an organization that provides an array of services for writers, both aspiring and professional, by means of presentations, workshops, contests, valuable net-working opportunities, critique services, and even awards prize money. Thank you all.

To all my fellow poets and writers who cheered me on, especially the *Fixed & Free Poets.* Write on.

To President, Steven Gamble, and Dean of the College of Education, Jerry Harmon of Eastern New Mexico University, who challenged me to pursue writing when I retired, I offer my thanks. I took your suggestion.

To all my fellow senior citizens who believe they are not too old to begin a new path, I say: Do it.

Locales

I am grateful to the helpful staff of the Tony Hillerman Branch Library, Hastings for inexpensive coffee, Einstein's Bagels, and various locations of Flying Star for unimpeded seat time, and Brennan and Kathleen Lucero, owners of Deli-Berry at whose front table I completed my first draft.

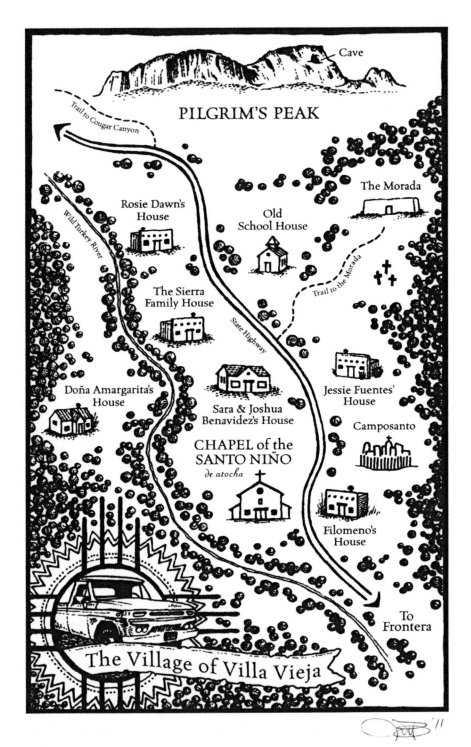

Map of Villa Vieja

Table of Contents

Incense and Beeswax
Villa Vieja, New Mexico, 1972

"I've never held a saint before," Ernie said as he cradled the 100-year-old carving of the Santo Niño de Atocha, the Holy Child. He held back the tears he considered unmanly, though a single one traced a silvery path down his leathery skin. As he stood in awe, he reflected on the twists and turns of the past months, events that had threatened the solidarity of the community of Villa Vieja.

The strange sequence had begun late one afternoon when Filomeno, the sacristan, was finishing up his duties. He had cleaned the chapel and was preparing to secure it for the night when he discovered that something was missing. Something desperately important.

Filomeno's aged eyes, encircled with wrinkled skin like a turtle's, adjusted to the dim light inside the small *capilla* dedicated to the miraculous Santo Niño de Atocha, nestled in a high mountain valley of *Nuevo España* in the village of Villa Vieja. Unextinguished candles gleamed, each with its tiny halo, atop the simple wooden altar. Filomeno, the sacristan, always checked twice to be certain that every candle was out before he left the chapel. The lush, lingering smell of beeswax reminded him.

The altar had to be arranged just so. He straightened the simple hand-embroidered altar cloths, picked up a crumpled leaf from the altar platform, and removed two dark brown beetles from the old wooden plank floor of the chapel. He checked that all the candles were out and that the *capilla* was in order.

As always, the sacristan knelt on the lower step of the altar platform to pay his respects to the Holy Child and ask for His blessing before closing the chapel for the night. He had one final duty.

With care, he arose and placed his foot on the top step of the altar platform. With his left hand, he held up the curtain that shielded the space beside the altar where the hand-carved image of the Santo Niño de Atocha was kept. The sacristan's eyes were no longer as keen as they used to be. He leaned in to check that the revered image was in its place. As he stepped up to the altar, he muttered aloud, "I got old man's eyes, gettin' all blurry." Filomeno reached his gnarled hand toward the altarpiece in front of him and swept it gently from left to right.

He felt nothing.

Disconcerted, he repeated the gesture from right to left. Still nothing, only space.

Dust motes drifted in slow motion through the disturbed air. The old sacristan gasped for breath. He stepped back in shock, almost losing his balance. Their precious statue was not in its accustomed place. *¿Por qué?* No one had mentioned borrowing it.

Filomeno turned away from the altar. "Where is your brother? Did you see anything?" he demanded of the blank-eyed, life-sized plaster Santo Niño that sat against the white-washed wall. The imposing statue, ornately dressed in bold primary colors, dominated the right side of the chapel. It remained placid and mute.

The sacristan had to tell the *mayordomos*, Joshua and Sara, right away. The elderly brother and sister were direct descendants of Old Mr. Benavídez, the *santero*, and their duty was to care for the chapel and all its contents. There had to be an explanation for the statue's absence. If not, *Dios mío*, if someone had stolen it, it would be very bad for everyone in Villa Vieja.

In Villa Vieja, it was the custom to allow the *gente* to take the statue home to pray a private novena for a special intention. Permission to borrow it came only from the *mayordomos*, Sara or Joshua, the elected caretakers. The borrower also had to inform Filomeno of the date of the loan and the date of its return. In a land where priests were scarce, the faithful had kept this special statue without harm for over one hundred years.

The chapel's tiny treasure was kept hidden in the custom-made pine box Old Mister Benavídez had made to protect it. The image nestled beneath the right side of the altar and was displayed only on special occasions. Carved of cottonwood root and painted with natural pigments in the 1870s by the area's best *santero,* the diminutive saint, about 12 inches high, rested in its box on a deerskin lining. A notched wooden bar latched into place across the seated figure's legs to keep it safe. The door was fastened with a leather thong. For over one hundred years the carved statue had been kept in good condition by the villagers. Only a few tiny paint flakes were missing.

Filomeno, knees shaking more than usual, looked up at the two genuflecting angels which bracketed the dome above the altar. What had they seen? Bent in adoration, with gracefully curved wings, the angels had kept their silence as long as the chapel had been the center of the village. With more than his usual care, he locked the deep blue door of the church with a long metal key. Beneath the midnight blue of the sky dome the first tiny stars peeped out.

The *mayordomos'* house was not far from the chapel. Filomeno scuttled along the dirt road as best he could on uncooperative legs, bowed by years of riding horseback. The moon was already up casting a silvery patina over the mountain valley. Cottonwoods along the river to his left were fully leaved, but cold still lingered in the canyon when the sun went down. A pair of owls called back and forth to each other from their perches. None of the dogs barked as Filomeno passed by. They all knew his smell and recognized his gait.

As Filomeno walked, he recited aloud the story of the Santo Niño. Filomeno loved the devotion brought to *Nueva España* from Spain and the accounts of miracles attributed to the Christ Child. Images portrayed the Santo Niño dressed in the style of a medieval pilgrim. The devout believed that the statue sallied forth at night to bring bread, water and comfort to those imprisoned or in great need. Most images portrayed him with chubby cheeks, happy and well-fed, with a basket over one arm, holding a staff with gourds filled with water. He sported a wide-brimmed hat with feather flourishes. This saint had *penache.* With ruffled collar and fancy cape, he appeared to be a rather dapper young pilgrim. Below the hem of his gown, the Niño's bare feet emerged. Filomeno called him *"el santo emplumado,"* the plumed saint, and chuckled softly. He always thought it was the vulnerability of those charming bare toes that made people love the little saint so much.

Because the Santo Niño walked about helping others, he wore out his sandals. In northern New Mexico, it became customary for people to give thanks for miraculous cures and answered prayers by leaving new sandals as an offering of thanksgiving. Even here in his own chapel, tucked away in this high mountain valley far away from his Spanish origins, the beloved image of the Christ Child was revered as protector and guardian by each successive generation of believers.

As he approached Joshua and Sara's house, Filomeno worried about how they would react. If the statue had been stolen, its disappearance would shock the community. Moreover, it would be a personal blow to Sara and Joshua. After all, their main duty was to keep the chapel and its contents safe. The answer had to be found right away. Filomeno knew how *mitote* could sweep through the village like an angry swarm of honeybees. One sting from a poisoned tongue could be deadly.

Filomeno unlatched the gate in front of the L-shaped adobe and walked toward the shadowed *portal.* Lights were on, so they were still awake.

The sacristan knocked at the blue door and waited.

"*¿Quién está?*"

"Is me," replied Filomeno. "*Es algo muy malo.*"

Joshua opened the door and gestured for him to enter. Filomeno's grey face signaled his distress. Joshua knew something had shaken this wise old man. "So, *amigo*, please sit down. Tell me: *¿Qué pasó?*"

"*Ay*, Señor Joshua, *gracias*, I need to sit down." He gulped a few deep breaths. The two men pulled out the often-painted chairs near the battered, wooden kitchen table.

Sara, Joshua's sister, heated up leftover coffee for them and waited. She stood with her back to them. Her grey hair was wrapped into a loose bun that was coming undone in spite of a number of black bobby pins stuck into it. She wore a simple brown dress was under her heavy, handmade wool sweater. Evenings were beginning to be cold. Her eyes appeared bluish, perhaps from cataracts. She had never been one to use makeup. Sara stood silent in the kitchen and kept quiet until spoken to.

"*Mana*, come sit down. Let's hear what news Filomeno has brought." Joshua patted the seat of the kitchen chair next to him.

"Is a terrible thing. I cannot believe." Filomeno stuttered out the news. "Someone has taken the little Santo Niño from the church. Is not there."

Sara gave a small gasp. Joshua's eyebrows shot up. Maybe Filomeno was mistaken.

"Are you sure?" Joshua knew that the old man's eyes were dimming.

"Is true. I pass my hands back and forth beside the altar where it 'posed to be. There's *nada*."

"Who else knows this?" Joshua's usually gentle voice was a bit sharp.

"Nobody. I come straight now from the chapel."

Joshua knew the old man's eyes were failing, so he asked Filomeno to stay with Sara. He grabbed a heavy, long-sleeved shirt from a wooden hook by the door and walked the dark road back to the chapel to verify the old man's story.

Joshua entered the back of the chapel with the new key and looked around the sacristy, his eyes adjusting to the low light. He opened every cabinet in the sacristy and looked in all the drawers where sacramental materials for the Mass were stored. Once inside the chapel itself, Joshua went straight to the space beside the altar where the Santo Niño was supposed to be. There was no sign of the little saint. Next, he checked behind all the handmade benches used for pews. He climbed the creaky steps to the old choir loft. He even peered up into the spaces under the rafters. From there, he looked down into the chapel. Nothing was out of place. With care, he descended the steep stairs and knelt on the altar platform.

"*Ay, Dios mío*," he lamented aloud. "It's gone." He said a fervent prayer to St. Anthony, the finder of lost objects, and headed back to his and Sara's house. It was unbelievable. Their beloved statue had vanished from its place beside the altar.

Hearing his steps on the porch, Sara opened the door and saw her brother's anguished face. The creases in Joshua's leathery skin appeared to have deepened. His dark brown eyes had hardened, like agate. She gave him an *abrazo*.

Joshua always turned to Sara for calm in the midst of storms. Sara motioned him to the table and brought the coffee pot. He sat down hard on the straight-backed chair and stared at the wood grain of the table.

"More coffee?" She lifted the pot.

Joshua shook his head.

"Think about what we do first," Sara suggested. "We need to tell as few people as possible and form a *comité*. Let's call the leaders together. Maybe someone saw something. Maybe it's just a misunderstanding." The two men nodded.

"Who should we invite?" Joshua's words were slow and spaced, like rocks falling out of a pickup bed on a bumpy road.

Sara knew who the leaders were. "For sure, we have to ask Doña Amargarita, the *curandera* and mid-wife. She knows everybody's business, not to mention their family history. And Jesse, the head of the *cofradía* – he has to come. Maybe Jay Sierra could come back to help. He's smart and cares about the *vecinos*. He would stay at his mother's house."

Sara's smile softened her gently furrowed skin as she mentioned Jay. Childless, Sara had longed for a son like Jay. He was only twelve when his father, Joaquin, had died when a tree fell on him while he was lumbering in the national forest. Sara had nurtured Jay as much as she could during those difficult years after his father's accident. His mother, Rita, had declined into solitude and depression and become a recluse. Sara admired the way Jay had taken on responsibility for his family, his younger sister, Susana, and David with the twisted leg, his little brother. People in the canyon had seen Jay mature into a fine young man. They respected him as an elder in spite of his youth.

"What about Rosie Dawn?" Sara asked.

"Why Rosie Dawn? It was probably one of her hippie friends who took our statue!" grumbled Joshua.

Joshua had never felt comfortable with the Anglo hippies who had invaded many of the small towns and villages in the area. He did not care for their laid-back ways and their so-called "free love" and drug use. The men wore long hair pulled back into ponytails and dressed like wannabe Indians. What kind of people were they? They painted their VW vans in psychedelic colors and lounged around under the pines weaving on their Eikel looms. They helped themselves to anything they saw even though it didn't belong to them.

The hippies didn't seem to care much for work, either, unlike the people in Villa Vieja who led hardscrabble lives and eked out a living from the land by working from early to late. The *vecinos* were tough and knew how to survive in this beautiful, remote, demanding place. What Joshua feared most was that their young people would be tempted to stray from their traditions of family and faith. Even now, it was hard to keep young people in the canyon. They could get better jobs and more education by moving to larger places. Worse yet, if they all moved away, who would care for the land, the animals, and the old ones?

Sara seldom contradicted her brother, but this time she spoke up.

"Rosie is not like the other hippies around here. When Mando abandoned her and her son, Harold, she stayed on. The others drifted away when life got too hard for them. Rosie's almost one of us now. She helps everyone, and even comes to Mass when we have it. I've heard she is devoted to the Santo Niño."

At the end of her uncharacteristically long speech, Sara folded her arms across her flat chest. Their cat, Gatito, climbed into her lap.

The men exchanged glances as they heard Rosie's defense. They both knew better than to argue with Sara who was as tenacious as a horsefly when she believed she was right.

"How about Ernie?" Filomeno ventured.

"Maybe, if we can't find the answer right away and get the statue back. God help us, we may need Ernie and the *policía* to help us. He'll come just as a member of the village, not as a cop, though."

Joshua chewed the inside of his lower lip the way he always did when he was anxious.

"What about Fr. Xavier Toledo, the one who's taking over for Padre Pedroso?" asked Filomeno in a tentative voice. The sacristan had been taught to respect priests, no matter what they did.

No one had met the acting pastor, but they had heard about his arrogance. It was hard enough to get a priest to say Mass any more. The Church could even close the chapel if the hierarchy found out the statue had disappeared.

"No!" fumed Joshua. "For now, leave the Church out of it. They don't need to know. We'll find our own statue. And as to Father Toledo, I don't know how that man calls himself a Catholic, much less a priest. From what I've heard, he will just talk, blame everyone else and listen to no one."

Joshua set his jaw. Both Filomeno and Sara knew any more discussion would be pointless.

They agreed to set the meeting for Tuesday evening after dark at the abandoned schoolhouse. They would contact the others right away. This secret had to be kept.

A Sweet Team

Jay Sierra tried to ignore the insistent ringing of the old black phone that was buried among piles of papers and books on a rickety desk crammed into a corner of his bachelor's apartment in Tres Cruces, a university town close to the Mexican border. When he was accepted at the Southwest Regional Center for Court Interpreters, he decided to enroll in a special one-year intensive program to train Spanish-speaking interpreters, of whom there were almost none in the area. An eager learner, Jay had quickly immersed himself in his studies. New responsibilities had complicated the methodical way he planned his days. The intrusive ringing upset his usual calm. He could not deal with any more disturbances today. Annoyed, he grabbed the receiver so hard the phone fell off the desk.

"Jay, here," he said.

"Hey, bro, it's Ernie. What's new with you?"

Jay was always glad to hear from Ernie whom he'd known from their first day in school in the big square schoolhouse in the village of Villa Vieja. After graduation, Ernie had joined the Police Department in Frontera, the largest town in the area.

Jay paused before answering his best friend. "Not much. What's up, Mr. Policeman?"

"Something has happened in the village. It may be a big crime and it could get complicated. I've never had to deal with anything like this. I'm going to need your help. What do you say? Drive up to Villa Vieja this weekend? I'll fill you in on what's going on when you get here."

"No way I can do that. I have obligations. I can't leave now."

"Come on, bro. This is big. We were always a great team, remember? Besides, you could visit your family, too," Ernie implored.

"I do need to check on my mom. Susana, my sister, says she's getting weaker. But I just can't get away right now."

"Listen, *carnal*. This is something that could rip the village apart. You gotta help me, not just me, the *gente*. The situation could get nasty. I want you here from the beginning, just in case."

"I am sorry, man, but I am tied down here."

Ernie wondered what was going on with Jay. They'd never kept secrets from each other. He sensed that Jay was withholding something, but he knew better than to push for explanations. Jay would tell him when he was ready.

"C'mon. It's only a seven-hour drive – you can do it," pleaded Ernie.

Jay did not want to disappoint his friend. They had always trusted each other.

"Let me think about it. If I can arrange things here, maybe I could break free for a couple of days, *no más*. I can't miss any classes. This program is really intense. Are you sure you really need me?"

"*Claro*, you know I wouldn't ask if this wasn't important. I'll explain when you get here. I owe you, man. *Gracias.*"

"See you soon, my friend. *Bueno*, bye."

Jacinto Carlos Sierra pondered what kind of emergency had caused Ernie Lucero, his childhood friend and cop, to demand his return to Villa Viejo pronto. Whatever the calamity was, the community must need him. Jay, as he was known, had refused at first, but he heard the concern in Ernie's voice. With reluctance, he had agreed. The necessary arrangements made, Jay filled up his truck with gas, threw his textbook of Spanish legal terms and a small gym bag behind the front seat. He put a few packages of peanut butter crackers on the front seat, slipped his favorite tape of northern New Mexico *rancheras* into the tape player and began the seven-hour journey to the mountains of home. He travelled back in time into a maze of memories.

As the big silver pickup he called Hi-Ho ascended the last hill studded dark with piñon and juniper trees, Jay felt a surge of excitement as he looked out the window toward the dusty, dun plains to his right. Soon he would see the distant blueberry outlines of mountains to his left. When, at last, he saw the familiar rise of Pilgrim's Peak, the majestic granite mountain that formed the backdrop to his childhood days, his lungs began to expand. His eyes gleamed. He could not hold back the tears that made thin golden streaks down his face. He was almost home.

Home for Jay was Villa Vieja, a scattering of modest dwellings constructed with adobe bricks plastered with a clayey mixture of mud mixed with straw. The simple houses were scattered along the winding canyon lined with cottonwoods fed by the small stream that meandered down to the foot of the canyon and spread out in a thin glaze over the sandy plains. Jay loved the peace of the evenings in Villa Vieja when bluish columns of smoke from wood stoves rose above the tin-clad roofs glinting in the last rays of sunlight. Light seemed to linger in the canyon, reluctant to leave. As a child, Jay loved to hear the old stories as he and his family gathered around the corner fireplace on cold winter evenings roasting *piñones*, cracking the hard brown shells between their teeth to extract the sweet pine nuts.

Jay's favorite tales were those about a holy man, the *hermitano,* who had lived for years in a small rock overhang near the top of Pilgrim's Peak. Like many, Jay saw in the peak's outline the profile of a supine man with a strong sloped forehead, an aquiline nose, and a smaller mound that suggested a chin. This constant visual icon reinforced the villagers' on-going memories of the holy man who had shared the valleys and mountains with them for four years. More than a hundred years after his departure, villagers felt blessed to dwell under the *hermitano's* holy presence. Man and mountain merged in their collective consciousness and fed the deep faith of the people.

Tall and slender, with high cheek bones, sea green eyes flecked with gold, bronzed skin, and black hair tied in a long ponytail, Jay could have been taken for a Spanish grandee, an Arab prince, a European noble, a Jewish scholar, even a Cherokee warrior. With his sensual full-lipped mouth and beaked nose, Jay was considered good-looking by all the *razas* who wanted to claim him. When asked about his heritage, he would smile slowly and say, "I'm New Mexican." He liked to keep people guessing. When he dressed up, Jay often wore a leather jacket with fringed sleeves, slim-legged jeans, and a silver *bolo* tie in the shape of an eagle inlaid with coral and turquoise. Topped off with an expensive leather hat, shaped just so, with a delicately beaded hatband, when he glimpsed his reflection, Jay had to admit that he was *muy guapo* – just as his younger sister, Susana, and her giggling friends whispered behind their hands.

With the back of his hand Jay wiped away the wet streaks from his cheeks. Responding to deep emotion "like a girl" was something he had tried to hide all his life. In his youth he had tolerated a lot of kidding from his buddies when his eyes filled and spilled over. *"¡Qué mariquita!"* chided his male companions, but the girls almost always thought it was cute that he cried.

Lost in reverie of the hermit and his birthplace, Jay almost missed the turnoff that would bring him to his favorite restaurant, The Star Café, in the small town of Frontera, on the border between the plains and the peak. He could barely contain his anticipation, or his hunger, for a huge plate of enchiladas (green was hotter this time of year), a cold beer (Dos Equis), followed by a basket of *sopaipillas* – puffed, fragrant fried bread shaped like little pillows, with warm honey melting down the inside. Even in Tres Cruces, it was impossible to get the tastes he craved, that distinctive northern New Mexico mix of flavors and traditional foods. Jay could wait no longer.

Jay squeezed Hi-Ho into a parking space near the entrance to The Star, smoothed his hair, adjusted his hat and hit the ground in a puff of dust. Shifting from one foot to the other, he polished the toes of his boots against his new Levis.

Would Ernie be there? Jay tried again to imagine what urgent matter had caused Ernie to demand that he come home. As he opened the door of the familiar landmark, he inhaled the aroma of enchiladas, pungent chile *salsa* and hot grease. Home again.

Jay noticed that the pressed tin ceiling was still intact, not painted over nor replaced. The red-topped seats at the old counter reminded him of the toadstools he and his friends used to find in the canyon after summer rains. Brightly decorated dish towels were tacked up on the walls and above the entrance. They featured real Mexican recipes and fetching *señoritas* wearing off-the-shoulder blouses and fiesta skirts. These linens were popular with tourists in the 1950s, and about as old as Jay. He glanced at the eclectic display of memorabilia from the owner's family that filled old glass-fronted cabinets along the walls. Colorful plates, Indian grinding stones, ornate old watches, turquoise and silver jewelry, and lumps of limestone embedded with fossils crowded the shelves. Small Japanese figurines, relics from sons who had returned from war, rubbed shoulders with cheap plaster saints. Below the high ceiling, serviceable tables and unremarkable chairs filled the plank-floored room. They had not changed since he was a kid. The Star was known for its food, not its décor.

Someone yelled just as Jay noticed an empty table toward the back of the room near the kitchen.

"Hey, *carnal*, what are you doing back here?" yelled Ernie, feigning surprise.

"Ernie, how's it going?"

Jay and Ernie gave each other big bear hugs, a few thumps on the back, and looked each other over. Jay towered over Ernie whose short legs and darker skin revealed his mixed Indian and Spanish heritage. Broad-shouldered and barrel-chested, sturdy, with black hair, unflinching brown eyes, and a square head, Ernie looked more like a *campesino* than a cop.

Jay gazed at his old pal, noting how he had aged. Squat, and with a bulging *panza* even in his uniform, he bore little resemblance to the athlete he'd been in high school. They had been a great combination, Ernie, the wide receiver and Jay the quarterback. They had anticipated each other's moves, and won plenty of games for the team.

How different their lives were now.

Ernie had married a girl from Frontera. They had two active children, a curly-haired boy of four and a straight-haired boy about three. Ernie took care of them on the evenings that his wife worked at a local bar. The patrons didn't mess with her when they found out her husband was a cop. The family lived in a mobile home on the edge of Frontera.

Jay had neither a career nor a wife. He felt as though he were losing ground.

"You're lookin' good, *hombre*," said Ernie as he appraised Jay's fancy duds. "Life down south must agree with you. Come join me and my buddies."

As Jay and Ernie headed toward the table in the back, several customers glanced sideways at Jay, spoonfuls of green chile stew suspended. Perhaps they wondered why one of their favorite sons was back in town. Word traveled faster here than a jackrabbit surprised by a coyote.

Jay shook hands around the table, recognizing a couple of the guys he had gone to school with. They had been lost kids from the *barrio*, and he guessed that these two hadn't traveled far from the junky old neighborhood. Nevertheless, it was good to see old acquaintances. Though anxious to know what had prompted Ernie's call, he'd have to wait until the jokes, the catching up, the beers, and the enchiladas were done to find out. In this part of God's universe, when the server asked "Red or green?" it had nothing to do with streetlights or Christmas.

After the younger men left, Ernie and Jay smiled across the table at each other, remembering all the adventures they had shared growing up in the canyon.

"How's the officer of the law doing these days in the land of the lawless?" asked Jay. Frontera had a well-deserved reputation as a town with an Old West mentality, even in the 1970s.

"Not too bad, all things considered," Ernie replied. "I know most of the families and who the troublemakers are. I try to set the kids straight, but if they break the law, I do my duty. Things are about normal for here. I like my job. I've even started preparing to take the exam for detective. I doubt I'll make it. How about you, Mr. Wannabe Court Interpreter?"

"I'm learning a lot. My Spanish is OK, but the legal terms are a challenge."

"How do you feel about defending the *mojados?*"

Jay was surprised to hear Ernie use a pejorative term for Mexicans who came across the border. Maybe Ernie was just trying to get a rise out of him. There was some friction between the families whose genealogies went back four hundred years and the recent influx from Mexico.

Jay paused before responding. He had majored in Spanish literature and knew about the issues facing Hispanics. He understood the concept of the *raza cósmica,* a term coined by José Vasconcelos, Mexican philosopher, to describe the positive *mestizaje* of European and indigenous peoples of the Américas as creating a "new breed of men." Jay felt that universality contained in his very own skin.

"I am fully aware of my heritage, bro, Indo-Hispano, if we want to get fancy. We are a *mezcla* of Indian, Spanish, other Europeans, Moors, and Semitic peoples. The *gente* around here still call themselves Spanish, not Mexican. We have our roots in Spain which incorporates many cultures. We just passed through Mexico on the way." Jay had assumed his professorial tone.

"Well, at least you recognize that we all have some Indian blood," Ernie replied. "Many of the *gente* won't even admit to their Indian ancestors. At least I know that my grandfather came from the pueblo called Cochiti."

Jay looked bemused. He and Ernie had had similar discussions before. Ernie had become active in the Chicano movement and was pretty knowledgeable about racism and discrimination, especially in northern New Mexico. For Ernie, the saving grace for the *raza* and a source of great pride for Hispanos was that they had held onto their land and retained most of their water rights, although not without some fights with the *gringos.*

Things were beginning to shift. The spillover from the Civil Rights Movement of the 1960s was beginning to trickle into New Mexico. Hispanos and anti-war activists began to fight for their human rights. Conspicuous by their absence in higher education, young Hispanos began to demand Chicano Studies courses. Since histories are written from the perspective of the conquerors, not the oppressed, Indo-Hispanos were virtually absent from the history books. The younger generation wanted to learn about their ancestors' contributions to history. By pounding on the portals of academia to demand admission and better access to higher education, they were beginning to find their voice.

The two old friends ordered cups of coffee and a dessert of sweet baked custard topped with a burnt sugar glaze. *"Muy rico"* was the verdict.

Jay leaned across the table and whispered, "So, what's going on in Villa Vieja that I had to get back here? What's happened?"

Ernie shook his head. "We can't talk here. It's serious. Meet me down by the bridge where we used to hang out. There's a picnic table there now."

Ernie got up, burped, paid the bill, and left. Jay followed about five minutes later. He put on his hat, greeted a few people he knew, and walked out into the night air.

Historia de las Historias

Jay parked Hi-Ho and walked down the slope to the river. Ernie was sitting at the concrete picnic table wearing the same old Stetson he'd worn for years. A medley of crickets rubbed their legs together, playing their evening song. A lone dog barked in the distance. They heard the roar of a low-rider as the driver gunned it over the bridge.

"So, why the urgency?"

"Nobody's told you what's going on?" A look of sadness softened Ernie's face. "The statue of the Santo Niño, the little wooden one, has disappeared from the chapel."

A quizzical look passed over the sculpted symmetry of Jay's face. "Is that all? Is that why you thought I should come back?"

"It's a big deal, bro. More than that, the disappearance is a *verguënza*. If something has happened to the statue, it will bring shame on the community. People won't feel safe anymore. They'll think that God has taken their protection away."

Ernie's agitation showed as he rose to his feet. He leaned across the table toward Jay.

"Something like this could destroy the community," Ernie added. "Everyone will become suspicious of everybody else. Worse yet, they'll feel that God is angry with them to let this happen."

Jay removed his hat and put it on the table. "What else?"

"I need your brains, Jay. I've never dealt with religious art theft. You, at least, know something about religious art. Didn't you take a class?"

Jay nodded. "Who knows about the theft now?"

"Old Filomeno, the *mayordomos* Joshua and Sara, me, Doña Amargarita, Rosie Dawn, Jesse, and now you. We're meeting Tuesday night at the old schoolhouse to try to find the statue before

Elizabeth Ann Galligan 17

the priest or anybody from the Church finds out. You're invited. There's no police report. Maybe it's just an accident."

"Ernie, I'm too involved in Tres Cruces to be here much. I have obligations."

Ernie knew that Jay was not telling him everything. No point in forcing the issue. What secret was Jay keeping from him? Jay would tell him when he was ready.

"*Bueno*. But this is a crisis, man. You and I were always a good team. We have different skills. Besides, Rosie Dawn lives in Villa Vieja with her son, Geraldo, who insists on being called 'Harold,' by the way. Wouldn't you like to get reacquainted?" He smiled and lifted an eyebrow.

Jay avoided answering Ernie's question as he tried to process what he had just heard. If he and Ernie were to lead an investigation, the situation would take more than a few days to resolve.

Ernie persisted. "It'll be better for us to work together."

When Jay looked at Ernie, Ernie saw that he had decided.

"Any leads, or should I say suspects?" Jay asked.

"Plenty. Some think it was outsiders, maybe the hippies that moved into Echo Canyon. Could be that raggedy gang from Washington State up in Beaver Canyon. Maybe they need money to get more heroin to sell. There have been lots of thefts around here lately. Possibly those *vatos locos* from the *barrio* in Frontera stole it. They just hang around making trouble.

"Besides that, we've got other problems. Did you know that somebody's stealing gravestones from the *camposantos*? Others steal saints from the churches and sell them for *mucho dinero*. That's really low. They disrespect our ancestors and our culture, man. Some people think it could be one of the villagers." Ernie looked at his old buddy with mute appeal.

"Why would anyone from Villa Vieja want to steal its most prized possession from the church? That Santo Niño has been in the chapel for almost a hundred years!"

"*Qué sé yo*? There could be lots of reasons. Maybe somebody's really angry at the Church, or thieves just want the money. ¿*Quien sabe*?"

"So, what do you think I can do right now?" Jay asked.

"Keep your eyes and ears open in Frontera. Most people don't remember you were the star student athlete. Maybe somebody will let something slip."

"OK, I'll be at the meeting," he said. "I'll try to see if I can find out anything. Good to see you, *carnal*." He gave Ernie a big *abrazo*.

"I've only got a few days. I've got to see how my family is doing," Jay said, as he rose, stretched and grabbed his hat.

"Oh, I almost forgot. Mando is around," Ernie added.

A series of expressions chased each other across Jay's face: surprise, curiosity, irritation. He squared his shoulders. Mando had been the village bad boy.

"Any idea why?" asked Jay.

"Not really. Keep your *ojos* open."

"OK, bro."

"*Bueno,* I'll see you at the meeting. As my *abuelita* used to say, *'En boca cerrada no entran moscas.'*"

"*Claro que sí.* I'll keep my mouth shut."

"OK, buddy. Take care. Give your family my regards."

"Same here. *Bueno,* bye."

Return of the Favorite Son

News traveled fast in Villa Vieja. When Sara arrived to tell Rosie Dawn about the statue's disappearance and invite her to the schoolhouse meeting, she mentioned that Jay was back and would be at the meeting.

"Do you know why he's here?" asked Rosie.

"I think it's because he's worried about his family."

"It will be good to see him again. How does he look?"

"Like a fancy cowboy, I think. But, you know, he is *muy buena gente.*"

Rosie smiled and said goodbye to Sara, accompanying her to the door. She had to bend her head to walk through the low doorway.

Rosie had rinsed her hands which were stained dark purple from the dye she was making for T-shirts to sell at the flea market in Frontera. Motionless, she gazed at the greenery outside the cabin. Memories rose slowly like the white clouds above the ridge line. No one could predict what those vapors would bring. Feelings long buried warmed her. She thought about what she would say to Jay when they met again.

Secret Keepers

After the cows were fed and birds had ceased their calling, one by one the *comité* began arriving at the old schoolhouse, a square building with thick walls made of adobe bricks plastered over with grey cement. Its tin roof was getting rusty. The school had been closed after the district decided to consolidate small rural schools into larger ones in town. All the *vecinos* at the meeting had attended the first five grades there. For some, that was the extent of their formal schooling. Children from Villa Vieja now had to rise early, even on frigid mornings, to catch the old yellow bus into Frontera.

Joshua led the meeting. He greeted each one as they arrived and indicated with a wave of his hand to sit down. If their saint had been stolen, they needed to find out who had taken it and why.

Doña Amargarita sat down her ample body at the foot of the table. Ernie glanced around and feigned surprise as Jay came in, smiled, and gave handshakes and greetings all around. Jesse noted with a slight grimace that the head and the foot of the table, places of importance, had been taken by Joshua and Doña Amarga, respectively. He chose the spot next to Ernie and across from Jay. Rosie Dawn hugged Sara, her friend, shook hands with the others, and chose a chair as far from Doña Amargarita as possible. Once the small group was assembled, Joshua opened the meeting with a prayer.

Dear *Señor Jesús*:

Look upon us with favor that we discover the unblemished statue of Yourself as the Holy Child so that Your image may return to its place in the village with us. Help us find the thief or thieves soon and bring them to justice for this sinful act. Do not let this *desgracia* travel beyond the canyon walls. We ask your Mother, the beloved Virgin Mary, to intercede for us. Amen. *Así sea.*

"Amen, *así sea,*" responded everyone.

Joshua cleared his throat, cracked the knuckles of each hand, and took a deep breath which sounded more like a sigh.

Before he could begin, Jesse blurted out, "How do we know that the statue is really gone?"

"We are here because Filomeno reported that the Santo Niño is missing from the chapel. After he brought the *malas noticias*, I myself checked the chapel and all the places it could be hidden. *Nada, nada.* Filomeno is right. Our little saint is missing.

"Nobody else but you here knows about this. We want to try to find out what happened ourselves. Now, do any of you know who has it? Did one of the elderlies borrow it without telling?" Joshua looked around the table at each one.

Ernie spoke up first. "As of now, we have no suspects and little evidence that a crime was committed. Couldn't someone have just forgotten to ask permission to take it home?"

Several people shook their heads.

Turning to Doña Amargarita, Ernie asked, "Who has had something bad happen to them recently or is upset?"

Doña Amargarita snorted. "This is Villa Vieja. Bad things happen here frequently – you know that. Just about anybody might need a favor from God. That makes everybody a suspect."

Rosie raised her hand and then quickly pulled it down, blushing. When Doña Amargarita was present, Rosie felt constrained. Gathering her confidence, she took a deep breath.

"How can we keep this quiet if we have to ask our neighbors about what they have seen or heard?" Rosie asked tremulously.

"Rosie's right," agreed Jay. "I think we need to see what we can find out – just us – by observing, without causing any alarm. If we don't know any more in a few days, we'll have to let the whole community know. Let's find out if anyone has seen something or someone out of the ordinary."

All nodded, rose from the uncomfortable chairs, said a Gloria, shook hands all around, and left. No one desired conversation. They had serious things to think about if they were to find out why the little saint had disappeared. Thunderclouds were gathering. It felt like rain. Distant thunder rumbled. Layered cloud banks above the rim of the canyon reflected pulses of light from sheet lightning. Members of the *comité* carried their perplexity home. Each had fitful dreams that night.

Town and Gown

From his vantage point on the second floor of the Humanities Building of Frontera University, Dr. Sheldon Parkhurst looked down upon the small town of Frontera, quiet in the hiatus between the end of summer classes and the beginning of the fall semester. To the west, he viewed quaint Victorian homes, some past their prime, and beyond them the cluster of adobe houses in the older and poorer section of town. To the north, the art history professor observed the campus of Frontera University centered on the Commons area.

Parkhurst crossed the hall and looked proudly at his name on the brass plate of the door to his office. He removed his color-coded keys from the pocket of his expensive slacks. No denims for him. He prided himself on dressing well – as the creased legs of his pants attested. When teaching, he wore a sports jacket and a *bolo* tie. A pity no one wears a suit any more, he clucked. He wore a freshly starched Arrow shirt every day, a habit that made him an avid patron of the local cleaning establishment. The shirt fit his slim body well. Pale hazel eyes looked out from fringed eyebrows of medium honey color. Although the sharp angles of his face could look almost sinister in low light, his facial features were well-balanced. Parkhurst thought himself reasonably good looking. His blondish hair was thinning. When he combed the longer hair back over the top, he looked pretty good for a bachelor approaching fifty. He couldn't resist taking another look through the huge glass windows at the campus and the surrounding town of Frontera. He walked back across the corridor.

The campus, golden green in the late sun, was at its peaceful best in the absence of the students, thought the professor. This was the time he most enjoyed his status as an academician, no papers to grade and no annoying students knocking on his closed door. In summer, he had time to work on the articles he hoped would bring him recognition and accolades, perhaps even a promotion.

Parkhurst looked down on the campus with satisfaction. The lawns were luxurious and untrammeled for the time being, empty of fast-food debris and carelessly tossed scraps of paper and cigarette butts. Trees burgeoned with their full measure of dark green leaves in late summer. Like concerned grandparents, the gnarled cottonwoods hovered over the edges of the Commons and seemed to long for voices of absent students. The lighter aspen trees shimmied their coin-shaped leaves in each slight breeze, full of energy like the young dancers Parkhurst had always fancied.

In the center of the Commons, breezes activated the movement of several kinetic mobiles that attracted Parkhurst's eyes. His predecessors in the Fine Arts Department had selected the outdoor art works that created visual interest. The mobiles were too abstract and angular for Parkhurst's taste.

Students liked to gather on the comfortable benches in the Commons to meet friends, eat sack lunches, check each other out, and flirt. Although the population of the small towns and villages of the area was primarily Hispano, few Hispanics felt welcome or invited into higher education. A visual survey revealed that the majority of the students were Caucasian. A negligible number of African-Americans and exchange students scarcely varied the whiteness of the students who found their way to this small bend in the river. In Parkhurst's opinion, there were too few real scholars of any ethnicity at Frontera University.

Hispanics had lived in the surrounding area for generations, but their sons and daughters were often not considered important enough to be educated. Families lacked the means and rural schools did not provide the preparation necessary for college success. In the jargon of the day, "political correctness" was based on demographics of the area, and the new Hispanic and native young people were "under-represented." Politically active Hispano youths had begun to call themselves Chicanos, a term that riled both Anglos and many longtime residents descended from the Spanish, who still called themselves Spanish. Traditionalists rejected the term *Chicano*, derived from *Méxicano*. Lines were becoming more sharply defined between and even within groups.

Ever since the mid-1960s the Civil Rights movement had brought the issues of ethnicity to the attention of the nation. Parkhurst thought the emphasis on ethnic identity a bogus one that would cause the "breaking up" of the America he knew. Even at Frontera University, students were beginning to demand ethnic studies courses. They wanted new texts, inclusive histories that honored all the area's peoples, both indigenous and new-comers. Their history did not begin with the colonists' story at Plymouth Rock. Roots of the *gente* sank deep into deserts and plateaus and had sprouted long before.

Face-offs between ethnicities over land had begun back when the Spaniards had simply claimed for the king the land belonging to indigenous peoples. Frontera had its own Wild West traditions of factions and conflict. Although conventional tensions between "town" and "gown" of the college people existed in many communities, in Frontera memories were long. Grudges and feuds lasted from generation to generation.

Parkhurst recalled a hallway conversation with one of his students, Enrique, a light-haired, green-eyed, fair-complected young man.

"People around here don't like outsiders. My fiancé and me – we're not from here. We're Hispanos, too. At the Rincón Bar, you know, where all the students hang out, they talk about us behind our backs in Spanish. We don't let them know we understand every word they say. Even our own families don't want us together, our own *gente*, because, sixty years ago, her great-uncle had a fight with my grandfather. People never forget a hurt around here. That's bad, man."

"Oh, excuse me, sir," Enrique had blurted in apology when he realized what he had just called his professor. Dr. Parkhurst indicated with a dismissive movement of his hand that the colloquial term had not bothered him. It was the first time a student had ever called him "man." He rather liked it.

Enrique's remarks had reminded Parkhurst that past grievances were seldom forgiven, and not just around here. A persistent frontier mentality invaded daily lives and entangled people in its snares. Parkhurst himself, an only child, had grown up in a wealthy suburb in Connecticut with all the privileges of a white upper-middle class family. He had little sympathy with students who felt that they were "victims." But, in the rare moments when he allowed his own childhood hurts and isolation as a teenager to rise into his consciousness, he knew again the persistent pain of past wounds.

Once, only once had he admitted his vulnerability – and then, only to one person. That bittersweet memory made him catch his breath. Suddenly, he saw his face, the former student he had confided in. And, he thought with disgust, that *pecadillo* could ruin my career. Parkhurst felt slightly nauseous as he stuffed down unwanted feelings that threatened to surface. If his secrets were known, his position might be in jeopardy. Nothing would prevent him from achieving a career and renown as a scholar.

Parkhurst took one last look out the big windows. From the plaza, he could hear the sounds of guitars and violas tuning up for the fiesta. Families gravitated toward the gazebo to watch the dancers. The professor watched couples join hands and make their way there. The tender beauty in the movements of the elderly couples, some who had partnered each other for fifty, even sixty years, touched him. He appreciated how they mirrored each other's movements in perfect precision. Old men sat on ornate but uncomfortable metal benches and gesticulated at each other as they argued about politics and the latest news. The same plaza where the musicians and dancers congregated had once been the scene of frontier justice. A plaque noted where the infamous "hanging tree" used to be.

The final image Parkhurst saw as he turned from the bucolic scenes below was of a three-story Victorian home with mustard yellow cupolas swelling above the tree line, a red widow's walk circling the roof. The house had been repainted a garish green. For some reason, he sighed as he turned toward his office. Enough procrastination.

Parkhurst opened the carved wooden door to his office, an extravagance for which he had paid out of his own pocket since the university did not compensate its professors for décor.

Parkhurst's predilection for Southwestern art was on full display. Custom-made bookcases with rhythmically curved decorations reached from floor to ceiling. Books on Southwestern art history and tomes of his own research, the effects of the growing tourist trade on the traditional market for Southwestern religious art, shared space with Hopi *kachinas,* micaceous pots that glinted in the sunshine, exquisitely decorated pots from various pueblos, and an unpainted, simple tree of life with animals and birds on every branch, carved from juniper root by José López, a carver. Several small Two Grey Hills tapestries he had bought from a Navajo weaver hung on the walls.

Not a religious man himself, Parkhurst had never understood the devotions and the fascination with the saints that were characteristic of the area. However, since he had chosen Spanish colonial religious art as his specialty, he was determined to become a recognized expert in the field.

The professor crossed to his large knotty pine desk, located his favorite pen, lined it up parallel to his notebook, and straightened a stack of papers that was slightly askew. All other stacks were perfectly aligned. He sat down in front of his electric typewriter to polish an article he was working on. He straightened his back, flexed his fingers, and turned on the typewriter. His deliberate movements were an effort to calm the agitation he felt.

He could not get his recent encounter with a former student out of his thoughts. The conversation had ended in a loud verbal confrontation. He shook his head to clear away the memory. He felt shaken and threatened by the possibility of serious outcomes for himself and his career. Small dark semicircles formed under each arm. His stomach sent rumblings of discontent. Parkhurst held his head in his hands and pressed his eyeballs with his manicured fingers. The only things he could see on the screen of his eyelids were amorphous shapes, black and yellow, forming and reforming.

Flower Power Blooms

Rosie Dawn listened to the noisy chants of "Make love, not war" on the boulevard below. She watched from her tiny veranda in a working-class neighborhood near the center of Los Angeles as throngs of long-skirted females with tie-dyed T-shirts and men with head-bands holding back their long hair marched down her street under a smoggy sky on their way to Griffith Park. Older than most of the protestors against the war in Viet Nam, she had not become involved. Although she opposed the war, Rosie made her protests quietly, behind the scenes. She was no longer part of the "youth of America."

She had become pregnant at sixteen and the baby's father had refused to take any responsibility. Rosie's own family kicked her out. She left Kansas and had struggled to raise her son, Geraldo – who insisted on being called Harold – alone. Through a series of menial jobs she managed to keep herself and her son fed and sheltered. She had tried to be a good role model. Rosie did not do drugs, and she surely did not want her son to use them. She sighed deeply. Just over thirty, Rosie felt worn down by the struggle of raising a boy-child.

Every time she caught a glimpse of her son, a tall, sturdy young man with long auburn curls any teenaged girl would love to have, Rosie Dawn was amazed. Harold was already a year older than she had been when she birthed him. Where had the small, quiet boy with big grey-green eyes and coppery red hair gone?

Tall and awkward, Harold was too shy be invited into any of the cliques in his California school, many of whom were Mexican-American or African-American. An outsider and newcomer, Harold didn't make many friends. He read science fiction and did well in school. In his spare time, he whittled small animals out of the wood scraps he picked up wherever he went. His carved pets kept him company. He sometimes made up stories about them. Behind their rented apartment, a wood pile provided Harold with all the carving material he needed.

Rosie, lanky, with deep hazel eyes, and fawn-colored hair, looked like the farm girl she had been. She rarely used make-up and avoided brilliant colors. She preferred natural fibers, earth tones, beige. With her long hair twisted into a bun held with chopsticks, and almond-shaped eyes, she resembled a pioneer, an American Gothic woman, stern and formidable.

One day when Rosie, nine years old, was playing jacks on the porch, she overheard her very own mother describe her to a neighbor as "plain as a mud fence." That one remark eroded her burgeoning sense of self and halted the arrival of any self-assurance. For years, the comment stifled her. Rosie left home as a teenaged mother vowing never to do harm to her child.

Although "growed up," Rosie was still hesitant to speak in groups. Her quiet demeanor, however, masked an agile brain and a quirky sense of humor that emerged as she developed trust. Rosie Dawn revealed herself faintly, like her namesake, and glowed brighter the longer one knew her.

By her own admission, Rosie was not a risk taker. But she had grown to like California. She admired the conviction of Californians who, native or not, rejoiced in adventure and risk. She believed that their freedom of spirit came naturally in a place where everyone clung to the edge of the continent, aware that they might, any day, fall into the ocean or sink back into the earth's magma. Californians embraced new ways of living. Perhaps she could become like them.

Today, she felt the urge to be a part of something larger than her daily struggles. She called out to Harold who was whittling a figure from the wood pile the landlord had said they could use.

"Come on, let's go down and join the march. I'll take snacks and we'll hang out in the park for a while." A mumbled grunt from Harold indicated that he would go.

As mother and son descended the steep hill to the street, one of the demonstrators asked Rosie to grab the corner of a banner saying,

"END THE WAR NOW!" Peace symbols filled the entire background. Rosie grabbed the corner. She knew better than to ask Harold to join in. He followed along the side of the street trying to look like a bystander.

The excitement of the crowd and the on-going chants lifted Rosie's energy. As the marchers entered the shade of the ancient live oaks in Griffith Park, amplifiers brought the sounds of impassioned speeches and the cheers of the crowd. They moved toward the podium to plant the banner.

Unable to see the uneven ground because of the banner she was holding, Rosie Dawn tripped and fell hard against the base of the podium. Slow to rise, she felt someone's arms from behind lifting her up. Slightly dazed, she looked into the man's eyes.

He grinned and said, "Well, *señorita,* don't feel bad. All the women fall for me," and gave out a deep hearty laugh. "Are you OK?" he asked.

Rosie, feeling flustered, answered, "I'm fine."

"And who is this fine young man?" he asked, indicating Harold who had come over to check on his mother.

"I'm her son," Harold said, scowling at the long-haired guy with fierce eyes and a red bandana around his head.

"Take good care of her, *mi'jo,*" the man replied.

"Call me Mando," he drawled and leapt back onto the podium. Rosie regained her footing and looked again at Mando who caught her eye and winked. She sensed his strength.

"Who is that?" she asked her banner partner. She wanted to remember those words forever.

"Oh, don't you know him? That's Armando Mares. Everybody calls him 'Mando.' He's one of the leaders of the movement."

Rosie looked up when she heard the usual "Testing, testing," accompanied by a loud breathing into the microphone. The speaker was Mando. She noticed his powerful thighs encased in well-worn Levis, his animal grace. The afternoon sun reflected in metallic sparks from a silver raven dangling on a shiny chain around his thick, sweaty neck. His eyes, bittersweet chocolate, held hers for a long moment. Then he took the mike.

"*Hermanos y hermanas*, it's wonderful to see so many of you here." He took another deep breath and began.

"It's time to end the war. It's time to make peace! We are the generation that can change the world! The system has held us down too long. We must take back our country and live our legacy of freedom. The man has held us down too long. We are the generation that must remake the country! Take back the White House! It's been white too long. Make the White House a rainbow house. Rainbow power will reign – black, brown, yellow, red, and yes, even a dash of white. No more discrimination. No more racist pigs. Take back the streets, take back the country! Make love, not war. Are you with us? Are you with us? I can't hear you! *¡Vamos a luchar!* How else can we achieve our birthright, our freedom? We have to take our country back. Nobody's giving it to us. Are you with us? Are you with us? Are you with us?"

Loud cheers crescendoed, echoing from the Hollywood Hills. Intrigued by her brief encounter with this man, Rosie felt a shiver of emotion she thought had vanished long ago. When the march broke up, small clots of people lingered in the shade of the twisted oaks, anxious to share the moment and anything else they had, food, flowers, marijuana, perfume.

"Hurry up," she urged Harold. "He's talking to some people. I want to thank him for helping me." They moved toward the podium. Then she pushed her way into the small group of marchers around Mando as he hunkered down on the edge of the podium. She noticed his T-shirt with the United Farm Workers' motto *"Sí, se puede!"*

"Thank you for aiding me when I fell. I felt pretty stupid. That was very kind of you."

"Will you fall for me again?" he asked, winking at her.

Rosie blushed. "It's been a long time since I've been knocked off my feet."

Friends of Mando called him over, and his attention shifted from Rosie as she and her son walked back into the shade and sat down. Rosie gracefully lowered herself to the grass, and with a demure gesture covered her long legs with her denim skirt. She hoped Mando would look for her at the next rally. She wanted to find out more about him.

To support herself and her son, Rosie had learned to weave. She earned welcome income at rallies and little stands by selling brightly colored woven items the hippies liked such as belts, beaded headbands, over-blouses, hair ties and guitar straps. Harold usually brought along his small carved animals to sell. He liked to make his own money, but Rosie was sad that the carvings seemed to be his only friends.

That evening, after she had turned out the light, Rosie did not fall asleep right away. Scenes from the march came to her in sequence like a slow-motion movie. The scene of her ignominious fall and the look and feel of those strong arms raising her to her feet kept winding and rewinding.

One rally led to another and soon Mando and Rosie Dawn became comrades at arms. One night, after long hours of running off flyers for the next rally on the ditto machine, they crashed on a convenient mattress at a friend's apartment. They made love. Mostly, they talked politics and held each other. Mando shared little about his own background and Rosie did not ask.

It wasn't until their second summer together that Mando asked a question that surprised Rosie.

"How would you and Harold like to go with me to visit the village where I grew up? The woman who raised me, Doña Amargarita, lives there."

"That's a great idea." Rosie replied. "I'll start saving for the trip." She wanted to know more about his early days. When she got back to the apartment, she told Harold about Mando's invitation.

"So, what do you think?" she asked.

"It might be a good idea. Where's he from again, Mexico?"

"*New* Mexico – it's a state," Rosie corrected. "We have to drive through the California desert, all of Arizona and about half-way across New Mexico. Want to go?"

Harold thought a trip might help him figure out what he was going to do with his life. Besides, he was more than ready to shuck his mother's preoccupations and burdens.

Rosie knew that Harold resented the time she spent with Mando. She had seen Harold sink into himself. He had his toe on the threshold of manhood, but he did not seem quite ready for it.

Rosie hoped, too, that the trip might lessen the tensions among them.

Rosie's Reveries

Rosie stood outside on the portal at the schoolhouse in the chilly evening. She knew everyone would want to talk with Jay after the meeting. Catching up would take a while. She and Jay needed to finalize plans for their trip to town to make quiet inquiries. As she waited, she thought back to her arrival in the canyon with Mando and Harold several years before.

Rosie, Mando and Harold had arrived in Frontera after a two-day, blazing drive from California in Mando's old pickup truck that was covered with slogans and peace symbols. Famished, they stopped at The Star for some good New Mexican food. Mando said he wanted to buy his foster mother a bouquet of flowers. Rosie smiled. She didn't often see Mando's softer side, and she liked it. They picked up a few groceries, a can of coffee, and a bag of beans for her. Harold spied a health food store, newly opened in Frontera. They bought granola, nuts, and some dried peas, suspecting that Doña Amarga would not have their preferred foods on her list of essentials.

Leaving town in the late afternoon, the three ascended a narrow road with lots of switchbacks that made Rosie feel sick. Harold loved the sharp turns and steep drop-offs, so he urged Mando to go faster. At least the air was cooler as they climbed toward the high mountain valley and Villa Vieja, the hamlet where Mando had grown up.

When they reached High Point, Mando pulled over.

"Let's get out. I want you to see this."

What Rosie Dawn and Harold saw was the breath-taking view from the cliffs extending all the way down to the plains. Dark green pines and scrub oak covered the slopes below them. Turkey vultures with trapezoidal wings surveyed them and lost interest. They were looking for road kill. An occasional red-tailed hawk glided above them. At the bottom of the canyon, splendid cliffs of pinkish granite bordered a slim silver thread of river that meandered toward small bright green *vegas*. Centered among the small scattering of houses in the narrow valley, an immense structure of purple-red sandstone with shiny turrets and spires planted its impressive girth. The building seemed misplaced, something from a fairy tale. Perhaps it was a mirage, an optical illusion. Beyond the edifice, limestone outcroppings stood as guardians. Then the plains began, immense, tan expanses of emptiness stretching away to the flat, hazy horizon.

"What's that in the middle? It looks like a castle!" exclaimed Harold, pointing.

"It used to be a fancy hotel, a spa, to house people who came to bathe in the hot springs down there. I don't know if you can see them from here. People say the water has healing powers," said Mando. "The Indians found these springs a long time ago. The villagers even say that the Aztec chief, Moctezuma, came here to bathe. That's one of the legends, anyway."

Harold's sharp eyes saw where little pools bubbled forth, each with white mists rising toward the sharp cerulean sky. "Can we bathe in the hot springs?" he asked.

"Sure, but not now. We got to get up the hill before it gets dark."

Tired of twisting, the road at last dropped into a high mountain valley. Small farms with bright cornstalks, rows of beans and vines heavy with squash bordered the river. A few scattered adobe buildings seemed to grow from the ground, rooted in the reddish brown clay.

Rosie noticed smoke drifting from a few smokestacks on tin roofs that reflected the late day sun.

"Why do they have fires now?" she asked. "It's summer."

Mando gave her his what-a foolish-question look and rolled his eyes.

"Lots of people here still use wood stoves. Doña Amargarita, my foster mother, swears by them. She'd never cook on butane. Says everything tastes better on a wood stove.

"By the way, she's 'Doña Amargarita' to you. She wants respect – and she deserves it," Mando cautioned.

Rosie pressed her lips tight and angled her thin body toward the window. Harold glanced at his mom and saw that she was embarrassed by Mando's jibe. Mando had a quick tongue and his comments often came out like put-downs. Harold knew that Rosie would not say another word until they arrived. He understood how she felt.

It had been Mando's idea to bring them to this forsaken part of northern New Mexico where he'd grown up. It was like traveling back in time about fifty years. Harold wondered what he was going to do for fun.

"Hey, Mando, when are we going to go hiking or ride a horse, like you said?"

"Soon's I find a couple of good horses for us. We'll go camping. I'll show you plenty. We might even see a bear."

"Cool." Harold gazed at the deep drop-off to the bottom of the canyon.

Rosie noted that she was not included in their boys' day-out plans. Harold had never been camping, so she was happy for him, but she wondered what she was going to do in Villa Vieja. She pursed her lips and folded her tensed hands in her lap, her usual response to small public blows to her self-esteem. Mando's public behavior was often in contrast to the lovely and flowery words he used when they were alone together.

"Does Amargarita – I mean, Doña Amargarita – know we're coming?" Rosie wondered aloud.

"Not exactly. She'll be happy, though. I haven't been to see her in, uh, maybe four years."

Rosie knew little about Mando's teen years before he had gone to Fresno State on a scholarship. "What was it like growing up in Villa Vieja?"

"I was a smart kid with a smart mouth. Everybody in the village knew I was an orphan and felt sorry for me. I got into a lot of fights. I didn't like being told what to do. Since I didn't have a father, I wasn't used to taking orders. So, I didn't."

"What about Doña Amargarita?"

"Doña Amarga was always getting called to the school when I messed up. She stood up for me, man. She told them her *hijito* wasn't a bad boy. *Fíjate.* She only finished the fifth grade and didn't have much respect for schools anyway."

Harold piped up, "So, how bad were you?"

"I'll tell you some other time," Mando whispered behind his hand, giving a sidewise glance at Rosie who smiled in spite of her pique.

"Did you go to high school in Frontera?" asked Harold.

"Yeah. *Tío* Tito asked me to come live with his family in Colorado. But I had a few friends here, and I didn't want to go so far away so I just stayed. Besides, Doña Amargarita needed me. It's hard for a woman alone here."

"How did she live? She was a widow, right?"

"No, she was an only child, and she never married. Her father taught her about native herbs and medicines and how to use them. Lucky for her, she's *muy inteligente.* She became the *curandera.* She's also the midwife. She delivers babies, helps with pregnant women and ones who want to get pregnant, and teaches them how to care for the *chiquitos.* Everybody knows Doña Amarga, and she knows everybody's business. People would pay her with stuff – eggs, chickens, corn, beans, a bag of potatoes, or a can of Snowcap lard. Sometimes they paid with cash. Then we got to go to town and buy a few things. I always got to buy an ice cream and a comic book. She fixed me up plenty of times with her poultices when I got in fights. She gave me teas for everything else, stomach aches, fever, even the runs. Man, some of that stuff tasted bad!" Mando made a face.

"She must be getting pretty old now. I'm glad we made the trip." Rosie smiled at Mando. Harold rested his head on his arm and looked out the window. All three of them grew quiet, enchanted by the view. Splendid thunderheads poked their blue-white bulges above the rim of the canyon and transformed into a series of shapes – angels, ice cream cones, charging buffaloes, an engine, and a head of cauliflower.

As the three ascended the winding road, the flora changed. Ponderosa pines, dark green scrub oak, and a few juniper and piñon trees clung to the slopes of the mountains. Early wildflowers bloomed, yellow flowers of different shapes and sizes, brown-eyed

Susans, New Mexico sunflowers with bright blooms spaced along their branches, yellow sweet clover, giant sunflowers with huge heads patterned with seeds that both birds and people loved to eat. Here and there, spikes of scarlet penstemon stood tall above a variegated carpet of color, plants with small white clustered blossoms, purple asters, flax, and the light-green fuzzy-leafed mullion.

When Harold saw clumps of dramatic orange-red flowers, like fire bursts, he pointed and called out, "What's that one?"

"They call it Indian paintbrush," replied Mando. "That one's my favorite."

"Cool."

Each of them felt the charm of the canyon and its tranquil effect. They rode for a while in silence. Along the river, sturdy cottonwoods lifted their massive branched arms. Below, riverbanks gleamed with the numinous light green of numerous willows. Fields of wheat bent their green heads, bowing to the breezes.

The three stayed with La Doña for the first few days. In her small house, she was matriarch. She refused any offers of help from "that *gringa,*" as she referred to Rosie who'd never even seen a wood stove before. She was no help, and Amarga treated her coldly. She secretly wondered whether Mando had fathered Harold. He didn't look like a "*coyote,*" the slang term used for mixed bloods, Mexican and white, but after Doña Amarga's years as the *partera,* midwife, bringing children into the world, she knew better than to speculate about their past lineage or their future appearance. After each birth she wet her thumb and made a cross on the newborn's forehead to protect the child from the *Ojo,* the evil eye. She knew how capricious genes could be. Red hair and blue eyes cropped up in families in northern New Mexico where one least expected them, as did very dark skin.

The *curandera's* house was hidden by trees near a bend in the river. From the first night they spent under her roof, Rosie saw that Amargarita clearly loved Mando and was not prepared to accept any contenders for her beloved "son." Rosie knew right away that Doña Amarga couldn't imagine this gawky *gringa* as his girlfriend.

As months passed in Villa Vieja, Rosie Dawn began to see a different facet of the complicated Mando. In California, he had been admired and sought out for his ideas. His pride in fighting for his *gente* gave him a radiance that inspired others. His face glowed when he spoke, and his words moved his listeners to action. When Mando stood at a microphone, he looked like a heroic bronze statue one might see in a park. He was accustomed to basking in the reflections of the hope in people's eyes as they determined to fight for their rights, for justice.

Rosie admired Mando's style and his forceful personality. In Villa Vieja, however, Rosie noticed that people drew away from him. After polite greetings, they would make excuses and leave. They avoided long conversations, especially about politics. They were suspicious of the radical movement through which Mando channeled his anger at the *gringos*. Other people did not agree with the Chicano militancy they heard about on the radio. Hispanos had a long history of submission and acceptance of their destiny. *Así es.* That's the way it is. God's will.

Perhaps they remembered Mando's wilder days as the "bad boy" of the village. Rosie began to sense that there was little connection to the place except for Amargarita. Thick walls, like those dividing the corrals from the barnyards, separated the old Mando from the new one. No one knew the man he had become, except Rosie.

Even Doña Amarga no longer knew her *hijito* the way she had. She was still proud of him, as always, and would defend him loudly to anyone who criticized him, but the boy she remembered, her *Armandito*, seemed to have vanished like piñon smoke in summer haze.

Because Doña Amargarita's house was small, Rosie and Mando often shared a tent in her yard unless the weather was bad. Together in the closeness of the canvas walls, Rosie felt stifled. Mando's size and force overpowered her. He reverted to the *macho hombre* that he was before. He became rough with her, physically and emotionally. He was the *jefe*. Rosie was used to bending like a willow in the wind.

One night the tension boiled over and struck like a mountain thunderstorm. "Move over, you are crowding me," grumbled Mando as he spread his barrel-shaped torso across the air mattress. When there was no response from Rosie, he became enraged.

"Get the hell over, *¡mujer!*"

Rosie felt a wave of emotion that had long been buried during the years she had struggled all alone. The anger she had suppressed at her rejection by both Harold's father and her family surfaced and spilled forth. A thick mass of bilious soup rose up through her stomach and spewed out her mouth, almost choking her.

"Don't you ever call me '*mujer*' again! I am not your woman. I am your friend and companion. What's happened to you, Mando? We were partners!" She was crying. Her hair flowed in swirls around her head. She was nauseous. Dry heaves racked her.

Mando grabbed her roughly in a half-tackle pinning her arms as well as he could as she flailed about. He threw her back onto the mattress.

"*¡Basta, mujer!* That's enough. You will never sass me like that again. I have had it with you and your pathetic son. You don't know your place."

As the storm subsided, they looked into each other's eyes and did not recognize what they saw. The storm-blasted tree of their relationship had destroyed their flower-filled days. In the after-surge, Mando and Rosie saw that their relationship had broken like a tree struck by lightning. Its burnt branches could no longer support their connection.

Mando pulled on his Levis and sweatshirt, grabbed his wallet and keys, and pushed his way out of the tent, hopping as he put on his shoes. The sound of the truck revving up told Rosie what she had suspected: that neither of them could forget their past hurts, and that being together, rather than soothing them, had compounded their fractures.

Harold had his own tent, too, and sometimes Paco stayed over with him. On those nights, they could hear the young men laughing and playing their music on their little transistor radios. When they heard the noise of the truck leaving, Harold got up.

He heard her sobs. If Mando never came back, Harold wouldn't shed a tear.

"Mom, are you all right?"

Rosie stood on the *portal* remembering those uncertain times. How ironic that Harold and I are the ones who stayed, she thought.

Stranded without a vehicle, Rosie had survived however she could. Like other hippies who had migrated to New Mexico in the early 1970s, Rosie found an abandoned house and became a squatter. No one ever asked her to leave. An old rusty bed, a rickety table, and some crates had served as furniture. She had her loom, and Harold had his carving knife. The two of them bartered items they'd made for rides to town where they sold their handiwork and made a bit of money.

Harold had made friends with Paco, a young man his age, who was Jesse Fuentes' only son. The two of them spent many hours together exploring. They learned about deer trails, bear caves, lookout points, where to catch the best fish, when to gather gooseberries and raspberries (in late summer). Harold and Paco disappeared for days at a time on their camping trips. Rosie received minimal information about their whereabouts.

Harold and Paco made costumes and acted out the stories they heard about Spanish settlers who fought back when Comanches and Apaches had raided villages. When there were rumors of a raid, it was told that the Spaniards hid their gold in caves. One never knew how true these stories were, but the possibility of lost treasure fueled the young men's desires to check out every cave and possible hiding place in the area. Rosie tried not to imagine what mischief they might get into.

The unexpected presence of Jay Sierra in Villa Vieja raised her spirits. She had missed her dear friend and wondered if they were still as close. Just then, Jay came out of the schoolhouse.

Jay left the meeting of the *comité* with mixed emotions. The placid memories of his childhood were giving way to the realization that Villa Vieja was no longer an isolated and forgotten village. People no longer waved at each other as their vehicles passed on the winding road up the canyon. He knew the community well enough to know the disappearance of the statue had to be solved quickly. Almost everyone had radios and phones now, so networks of rumor and gossip could travel even more quickly than before. But, when it became necessary to keep a secret for the good of the community, a Mafia-like code of silence prevailed. Although concerned about the changes creeping to Villa Vieja, Jay was happily anticipating spending time with Rosie. They would have little of it to rekindle their relationship.

Jay and Rosie hugged. "Sorry it took so long, Rosie. I had a lot of people to catch up with."

"It's OK," she replied. "The stars are beautiful tonight. It's a good time to think about things. It's so nice out I think I'll walk home."

"*Bueno*, I'll pick you up in Hi-Ho at your *casita* about 7:15 tomorrow morning."

"Great. I'll be ready."

Jay drove to his mother's house. In quiet darkness under a spill of stars so thick the Milky Way looked like a river of diamonds sparkling across the velvet sky. Jay and Rosie both savored their encounter and anticipated the next.

Tres Amigos

Jay was right on time the next morning. The road to Frontera had many switchbacks in its 13 twisting miles, so it took about 20 minutes to get to town.

"We don't have time to waste. Let's get started," Jay suggested without the usual preliminary courtesies, perhaps masking his delight in seeing Rosie Dawn again.

"My family mentioned you when I saw them. They told me you had become *como la gente*, one of us."

Rosie smiled. "I do see Susana from time to time, and we talk. I like her. Your sister is growing into very capable young women. How is your mother doing?"

"Still reclusive. She has never gotten over my father's death. She almost never talks, from what Susanita and David tell me. You know she never leaves the house, so Susana really runs the home. David is pretty limited in what he can do, but he gathers wood and takes care of the animals. He has a pet chipmunk that he caught. He is good with animals. I send them some money from time to time."

A flush of sadness gradually washed over Jay's well-sculpted face. Rosie looked discretely away when she saw his gold-green eyes welling with tears. When he looked at her, his eyes reminded her of the ocean at twilight, deep and sparkling. It was one of the things she missed about California, or was it really California she missed?

"I can't believe you're still living here. How's Mando?" Jay asked.

"I don't know. He left a long time ago. Nobody has seen or heard from him."

"Not even Doña Amarga?"

"La Doña wouldn't tell me if she knew. I don't think Mando could dispel the bad memories of being an orphan, a *pobrecito*, an outcast. He still harbors a lot of anger and pain, and people here seem to be stuck in their attitudes. In California he was known as one of the head *honchos* of the Chicano Movement and got a lot of respect. He channeled his anger at the *gringos* and began fighting for his *gente*. When he came back here, he was still seen as that bad boy who had caused so much trouble. He wasn't welcome. So, he got really depressed and withdrew. We had a huge fight, and he just roared out of here one day in the truck, so Harold and I were sort of stranded."

Jay didn't mention that he'd heard that Mando was back in the area. He decided not to bring that up now. "So, you just gritted it out and stayed. I'm impressed. How's Geraldo – oops, Harold – doing? He must be almost grown."

"I worry about him sometimes. You know how young men are." Rosie replied. "He's almost eighteen, but he hasn't quite jelled yet. He's still trying to figure out who he is and what he wants to be. He and Paco, Jesse's son, are best friends. They told me they were going to camp in Cougar Canyon for a few days. I don't know what they're up to. I think Paco leads that boy into mischief he wouldn't get into by himself. It's sad. Harold has never had a best friend until Paco." Rosie took a deep breath.

"He'll turn out OK. Look at his mom." Jay's compliment warmed the evening chill. Rosie felt that someone had gently placed a comforting shawl around her thin, strong shoulders. She smiled and dared look into those sympathetic eyes again.

"So, Doña Rosie, what's the plan? You're more familiar with the artsy-crafty scene than I am."

"I think we should check with Ernie in town and find out if he has picked up any leads. Then, we'll visit some local dealers who collect or sell religious art. We don't want to be too obvious."

"What about asking around at the university?" Jay asked.

"Too soon. Word will get out. Besides, everyone knows you there, unless you're planning on going in disguise?" teased Rosie.

"Will you?" Jay retorted.

"It's pretty hard to go unnoticed when one is 5' 9" tall, and an Anglo woman."

They both laughed. How quickly they had fallen into the teasing banter they had always enjoyed.

Jay knew just where to look for Ernie at this early hour – at The Span. The landmark was a gathering place popular with students, locals, professors, politicos, tourists, and anyone who wanted a place for *negocios*, legal or illegal. If one wanted to find someone in Frontera, the first place to look was The Span. Its name might be an historical reference to the bridge that had long divided Frontera into "Old Town" and "New Town." More likely, it was a reference to how one's clothes fit after too many hearty meals and their home-made donuts. In Ernie's case, it was the latter.

Sure enough, Rosie and Jay found Ernie in a booth toward the back, platters spread across the table filled with his ample breakfast of huevos rancheros, tortillas, *papas fritas, salchica,* and a big mug of good, strong coffee.

Ernie waved and motioned Rosie and Jay to join him. After he gave Jay a hug, Ernie opened his arms toward Rosie. She blushed and gave a stiff-armed semblance of an embrace to Ernie who was about three inches shorter than she. Public displays of affection were not her style. Ernie shot a raised-eyebrow glance at Jay that seemed to ask, what did I do wrong?

Rosie and Jay ordered. They compared notes with Ernie about the meeting the night before, the need for secrecy, and ideas on how to proceed.

"Are there any dealers in religious art suddenly doing a good business? Any newcomers who might not be on the up-and-up?" Jay asked.

"I haven't heard anything at the police station and I checked around," Ernie said. "Did you know that we've had lots of thefts lately of all kinds? Remember when people just left their tools lying on the ground, and nobody locked their doors?" He shook his head. "It's not that way now. Some blame the thefts on the hippies. They come here in their fake Indian outfits and beads and 'liberate' anything they see and want. Just because it's there. What kind of *educación* do they have? No respect. Can you believe some of our grandparents' gravestones are disappearing from the *camposantos*? Disgusting." Ernie patted his expanding *panza* and burped.

"Can they sell these things? Who would buy something like that?" asked Jay.

"You'd be surprised. There are dealers who want Southwestern folk art because it's different. They can find buyers for big bucks. It's in. Others just sell things to get money. As to religious art, neither the dealers nor the buyers have a clue as to why it's wrong to remove sacred objects, but that's what they are. They've never heard of sacrilege. If they want something, they think they should have it. Values and ethics go right out the door.

"Be careful when you ask around, bro," Ernie warned. "Word travels faster than a hungry coyote after a baby rabbit around here."

"OK, *amigo*," Jay replied. He gave the still-seated Ernie a half hug. Jay gave Rosie a thumb's up when he saw her bend down to hug Ernie, too.

As Rosie and Jay neared the counter, they spied homemade donuts under the glass. They nodded at each other, yes. They chose the flavors with care and started eating their donuts before they got out the door. Just like old times.

As they left, Jay noticed an old professor of his in a back corner leaning into an intense conversation with a dark-haired, powerfully built man he could see only from the back. Something about him seemed familiar.

"Let's get started and see if we pick up anything," suggested Jay.

"I know Victor Vigil. Let's go there first. He's been selling religious art for years and years around here, and he knows most of the *santeros*. His shop's not far," said Rosie. "Besides, he may have some money for me. My weavings sell well there."

"Oh, becoming a capitalist now, are you?" Jay jibed.

Rosie just smiled.

Around the plaza, many of the old storefronts that used to display Levis, boots, and Communion dresses had been converted into places that attracted tourists. A health food store had sprung up there featuring the fancied-up oats the hippies called granola. One could buy tie-dyed T-shirts in another. A "head shop" featured drug paraphernalia. Frontera boasted one bookstore that prospered as an oasis of literary culture, a magnet for anyone interested in good literature or Southwest history and culture. Customers included professors and students from the college as well as townspeople. Jay was pleased to see that the bookstore was still in business. He would go in and chat with the owners the next time.

Jay parked Hi-Ho nearby and locked his backpack inside a metal box in the back with shiny waffle-shaped designs on it. Since Jay had bought the pickup in Tres Cruces, no one would recognize his vehicle. There was no need to tempt the *pobrecitos*, the loiterers and the mentally unstable people who wandered around the town. They were a fixture in Frontera. Jay even recognized some of them from years before. They seldom caused much trouble, but one always needed to be careful. He smiled, wished them a good day and kept his *ojos* open.

Rosie preceded Jay into Galleria Victoria.

"Ah, it's a rosy dawn to brighten my day," exclaimed *Señor* Victor Vigil. The shop owner was a short heavyset man with shaggy eyebrows, a broad flat nose, russet cheeks and a hearty smile. His warm brown eyes crinkled when he saw her.

Rosie blushed and held back slightly as Victor came from behind the counter and enveloped her in an avuncular bear hug. Would she ever get used to these public displays of affection? Rosie did not think so.

Victor looked Jay over for a moment before he recognized the handsome young man with her, then shook his hand. "Jacinto, what are you doing here?"

"I just came for a short visit to see my family and to take care of some *negocios,* Señor Vigil. How's business these days?" Jay was always reserved and courteous with his elders even though he was no longer a youngster, and no one ever called him by his given name.

"We just came in to say hello and see what wonderful things you have in the store," Rosie said.

"Well, look around. By the way, Rosie, I have an envelope with your name on it. Would you like it?"

"Sure," she smiled. That people paid real money for her weavings pleased her greatly. The sum was more than she expected. She would buy some skeins of the special wool she liked. For Rosie, splurges were rare. She carefully tucked away the envelope in one of the large pockets of the patchwork skirt she had made herself. When she approached it, Rosie was pleased to see that Victor had displayed her weavings close to the counter where everyone could see them.

"When are you going to bring me some of Harold's carvings? People like those little *animalitos* he makes."

"One of these days. You know, he's at the age that no one can tell him what to do, especially his mother."

"He's a good boy. He'll turn out OK," reassured Victor.

Jay scanned the shelves filled with old and new art works with prices that ranged from reasonable to exorbitant.

"How's your family? Business going well?" asked Jay.

Victor paused for a moment and pursed his lips as if considering how to respond.

"Some days good, some days not so good. You never know. Once in a while, somebody brings in something different. The other day, one of those long-haired *gringos* came in and said he wanted me to buy some things in his truck. So, I go out and what has he got? Old wagon wheel hubs, some rusty tools, a washtub with hole in it, and a headstone. When I saw that headstone, I told him to get the hell out of here or I would call the police and accuse him of theft. He peeled out, black exhaust pouring from the back of the truck like a skunk spewing its smell. I don't know what's gotten into people. How can they dare to dishonor the dead like that? God deliver us! I've heard other shop owners have had similar experiences. We don't want those long-haired weasels around here."

"Why would anyone buy something like that?" queried Rosie.

"*¿Quién sabe?*" replied Mr. Vigil. "Nobody who has any *educación*, but, you know today, some people just not are raised to respect others. It's the times, I guess. Sometimes museums buy stuff like that. Some call it 'popular culture,' you know, like folk art. Maybe those rich Anglos set up the gravestones in their fancy gardens. If they do, I hope the souls of the departed don't let any of those buyers rest in peace. It's supposed to be 'cool' now to have a piece of folk art. *Muy frío,* I'd say."

All three laughed at Victor's joke.

"Well, you did the right thing, Mr. Vigil. That guy won't come around again." Jay found Rosie looking at a shelf filled with jewelry of semi-precious stones and turquoise and silver, the kinds she liked best.

"*Bueno*, we'd better go," Jay extended his hand to Mr. Vigil. "It was great to see you. *Cuídate bien, Señor.*"

As they left the gallery, Rosie realized how much her life had improved. She had new friends, sold her work in Frontera, and had found people she loved and admired. For the first time since she left the Midwest, she had found a home called Villa Vieja.

Back in the truck, Jay and Rosie discussed the encounter with Mr. Vigil.

"He's a fine man, but I don't know if we're getting anywhere with this," Jay commented.

"Let's drop in on a few more galleries. I think if they have heard anything, the owners will tell us," suggested Rosie.

"OK. When we finish, how about another donut and some coffee at The Span?"

"That sounds good to me, mmmm," said Rosie licking her lips in anticipation.

By the time they finished their survey of the galleries, they had no leads, but the donuts were delicious, as always.

As they left for Villa Vieja, the sun was disappearing behind the mountains. Afternoon thunderheads had not kept the promise of rain but were forgiven as they glowed in rosy beige scoops, changed to pink amber, and then to fuchsia. The light lowered. Every living thing was bundled into the soft shadows of the night.

Jay dropped Rosie off at her modest little house near the village. She asked him to come in for a cup of hot coffee, but he demurred. He needed to be alone to mull over the alleged theft of the santo, the needs of his family, and his next steps.

Cottonwood Ponderings

Jay drove Hi-Ho a short distance and parked in a wide shoulder where a huge cottonwood overhung the road. How well he remembered that wonderful old tree. He paused beneath its sheltering branches and grabbed a snack package of cheese and peanut butter. The moon was so bright he had no trouble hoisting himself into the lap of the tree he had climbed many times as a child to his secret place of solace and support. He balanced himself by placing his long legs against two sturdy branches. The cold air was still spiced with the hint of piñon smoke. The ponderosas gave off their own fresh scent. He leaned against what he had always called his "thinking tree." His thoughts were running pell-mell like goats headed home. He needed to corral them before he went back to his mother's home. He knew he would be pulled this way and that, like an unruly horse by the reins of his family.

Where should he put his energy? Could he be of any help to the village or to his family? It was hard being so far away.

Jay's approach to problems was to deliberate alone, examine all points of view, then draw his own conclusions. What was probable was that the statue was gone. It was still possible that it was not a theft but simple mischief or a lapse of memory by one of the *viejitos*. Jay wondered why someone from the village would commit such a desecration. That was the most perplexing part. For over a hundred years, the little statue had been safely housed in the small *capilla* that served both as chapel and as a community meeting place. The Holy Child loved Villa Vieja and the people loved the Child who protected the village. What would compel anyone to risk His ire?

It must have been outsiders, thought Jay. There were the usual suspects – *vatos locos* from Frontera who needed money for their drug habits, any one of the hippies who still stayed on the fringes of village life, some who seemed to have no ethics or respect for the villagers, their property, or their traditions. In this area, whenever anything went amiss, it was common to blame escapees from the mental hospital. As much as Jay disliked the idea, the guilty party could even be a priest, perhaps jealous of the autonomy of the *capilla* and its governance by the community. The *vecinos* did not always depend on the hierarchy for their spiritual practices. People from Villa Vieja practiced their faith and took care of their own, with or without priests.

On the other hand, someone must have had access to a key. The windows and doors were intact. That suggested insiders or, at least, someone familiar with village life. How did they get the key? Someone close to the Church must have been involved. Maybe the head of the *cofradía* or a villager at odds with the church? Who else had a key? How did the thieves manage to remove the statue? Where was it now? Nothing was clear as of yet.

Seeing Ernie, Rosie, his family, and his *gente* made Jay realize how accustomed he had become to being alone, keeping his own counsel. He could easily become a hermit, he sometimes thought. Maybe he would go and live in the hermit's cave in the nearby peak for a summer. At least, there was a precedent. A tiny smile crept onto his lips and he laughed at himself. Jay hadn't realized how much he missed his people and the comforting familiarity of the river, the mountain valleys, and the sky, oh, yes, the sky.

OK, time to make some plans. Jay climbed down from the huge comforting arms of the ancient cottonwood with a clearer idea of what he had to do. He decided to leave the day after the open community meeting at the church. He had come back to Villa Vieja not only as a leader, but because his family needed his help.

Tonight Jay would enjoy his family.

Jay, Susana, and their brother, David, played cards and talked. The fire in the wood stove gave out welcome warmth, and the siblings roasted a few *piñones* and visited until the last coals turned into soft ashes. They gave each other hugs and wished each other good night the way their mother always used to before they went to bed.

"Duerme con los angelitos."

"Igualmente."

David wondered what was so great about "sleeping with the little angels" but he remembered when his mother used to tuck him in and make a small cross on his forehead. He always slept better then. That was before his mother had retreated from them, shrouded in her own tightly bound confinement.

Jay wrapped himself in blankets and lay down on the lumpy sofa. He had to prop his feet on the arm. He had grown too tall for it by the time he was fourteen.

Before he fell asleep, Jay wondered about Jesse. He was surprised to hear that Jesse Fuentes had become one of the leaders of the village and was elected *hermano mayor* of the *cofradía.* Jay had not known Jesse well although they were almost the same age. The Fuentes family had moved to Villa Vieja just after Jay's father had passed away. Jay was involved in helping his own family survive. He had no time for fun. Jay would try to learn what Jesse knew about the disappearance. In the peaceful dark, a coyote yipped in the distance. The valley shut down for the night. A medley of stars sprinkled the night sky.

The next morning, Jay hung up the phone to find his mother standing behind him. Rita, who seldom spoke, murmured, "Why are you going so soon, *¿mi'jito?"*

Jay turned and hugged her frail shoulders. "Don't worry, *mamá.* I'll be back in a couple of months to see you. Don't worry. You take good care of yourself. *Cuídate bien."*

When Jay noticed two small tears oozing from her rheumy eyes, he mirrored her tears with his own. His mother shuffled out of the kitchen in her fuzzy slippers and returned to her room. He turned his face away so that Susana would not see the tears. His sister looked at his broad shoulders sadly. Her big brother had always been more like a father to her. She hated that he was going to leave so soon.

"When will you be back?" Susana asked.

"In about two months – I'll be back for *La Nochebuena* and Christmas."

Susana sighed. Jay smiled at her and held her shoulders.

"You are a good daughter and a wonderful sister. Take good care of them."

She inclined her head and rested it on Jay's chest. Susana felt almost as she did when the priest blessed her. Praise from Jay made her feel special.

Jay and Susana were almost mirror images. Susana had lustrous black hair that she wore tied back with ribbon. She had the same light skin tones as Jay. Her features were symmetrical, more delicate than his. She also shared his slightly hooked nose and high cheekbones. Only the color of her eyes, a velvet brown, set into an oval face like a cameo, was different. Susana was as beautiful as Jay was handsome.

Susana was relieved to hear that Jay would be back soon. She had taken on the responsibility for her mother and brother, just as Jay had become the head of the family when their father died. Her friends had graduated from high school and were beginning their "real lives." She had put her hopes for her own future on hold. She knew that Jay would help her get a good education. She hadn't decided whether to be a nurse or a bookkeeper. With her experience in running her mother's frugal household, she felt she would be good at either. And she was learning how to cook. Maybe she would open a restaurant someday. She felt her life had not begun. Susana was anxious to become her own woman.

Jay was unloading a 25-pound bag of beans he'd brought for the family when, with surprise, he saw Jesse striding up the path on legs longer than his own. Jesse's usual Dallas Cowboys cap could not contain his mass of coppery curls. His ice blue eyes in his long horse-face were startling. With skin the color of dark honey and a long thin nose, Jesse looked like a stranger – an outsider. At 5' 11" he was taller than most of his buddies. He's almost as tall as I am, Jay noted. When he saw Jesse's long, sinewy arms and tall stovepipe legs, "the better to run away with," he recalled how Jesse was teased by the other boys who nicknamed him *espantajo*, "Scarecrow." Jay guessed that Jesse hated the name, but he had to go along to be one of the guys. He needed friends. You have to give him credit, thought Jay. Treated as a misfit, he used the challenge to overcome his shyness by reaching out to others. Now he was a leader in the village.

Jay went out to meet him, eyebrows raised. He reached out to shake his hand.

"*¡Hóla!* Jesse. What's up?"

"I just wanted to check in with you. Joshua's going to call the people together tomorrow at three o'clock by ringing the chapel bell. Then he'll ask them if they know anything. If nobody speaks up or is afraid to say anything, we'll just start the *Novena Dedicated to the Most Miraculous Child of Atocha* right away. It'll continue for nine weeks. Maybe that will get us some results. After all, the Niño wants his statue found, too, *¿qué no?*"

"*Claro que sí.* Have any ideas?"

"Not really. I'd hate to have to tell Fr. X. I never met a priest like him before."

Jay wondered if Jesse really had met the priest, or if he was name-dropping to sound important. He let it pass.

Jay promised, "I'll be at the meeting tomorrow, but I've got to go back in a day or two."

"OK. I don't know how much you can do from there." Jesse said.

"Me, neither. But I've got some ideas about how to find out the truth. I'll work with Ernie. He'll keep me posted. I can do some research about local shady dealers in religious art. I'll start with Tres Cruces and then check out southern California."

"As long as we find out the truth." Jesse strode down the path, thoughts whizzing like flies around this head.

"See you, Jesse. Thanks for coming by. We aren't supposed to do anything yet, just wait until the 'emergency' meeting?"

"You got it, man."

"OK. *Hasta.*"

Jay did not know Jesse well. Jay had been too busy helping is family to hang around with anyone except Ernie. He decided to find out more about him.

Later that day he walked to Sara's house for a visit. He felt strong affection for the woman who had been so kind to him when he was young. After the customary greetings and small talk, Jay asked, "Doña Sara, tell me what you know about Jesse Fuentes."

"*Bueno*, his family moved into the village in the 1950s. You know that it takes the *vecinos* a long time to be welcomed here, to be considered one of the *gente*. After all, some of our families trace their roots back over four hundred years. They were viewed as outsiders.

"I think Jesse could never forget the awful feeling he had when his parents decided to move to Villa Vieja. He was skinny, like he didn't get enough to eat, and very shy. The other boys teased him about his hair, his looks, and his height. He always liked the church, even as a boy. I think the church is the only place he felt safe. It gave him a haven. He always offered to help the sacristan or even the ladies who clean the chapel. There he was accepted. His family never liked it here. When they moved away Jesse stayed on in the village by himself. He found odd jobs. I think Filomeno even took him in for a while before Jesse found a little shack to live in."

"I never heard that before. He had it pretty rough, I guess," said Jay.

"Jesse had to grow up quick. He fell in love with Carmela, a girl from here. He fathered Francisco (Paco) with her. Her parents were *muy enojados*. She delivered a perfect, healthy baby, and Jesse wanted to marry her, but Carmela's parents opposed their daughter's desire to marry him. He was still considered an outsider without roots. They insisted that Carmela and her son, Paco, live with them. Carmela was sickly – how do you call it? – a blue baby with a weak heart? Doña Amargarita saved her life when she was born. Her parents were always very protective.

"As time passed, her parents saw Jesse's sincere devotion to their grandson. They began to appreciate Jesse as a serious young man. Somebody helped him get a job with the state highway department. Since Jesse worked days in road construction, Paco remained with his grandparents. Jesse saw him every day.

"When Carmela, *pobrecita*, died at twenty-two, it was very sad. Jesse lost the love of his life and wanted his son with him more than ever. Paco stayed on with his grandparents when Jesse had jobs. Sometimes he spent the night with his father. When he was eight, Paco moved in with his father for good. They are very close, like rice and beans."

"I appreciate you telling me. Everybody's got a story," observed Jay.

Sara gazed at him and they exchanged a look of deep affection. They sat and sipped cups of *yerba buena* that Sara had brewed.

"One more question, if you have time. Are Jesse and Rosie close?" Jay wondered.

Sara was not sure why Jay was asking about Rosie.

"*Pues...*" Sara paused. "They are both, how do you say, 'singles?' That's not common here. Since Harold and Paco are best friends, maybe they talk about their sons. It's nothing more than that."

"It's hard for a woman by herself here, I guess. Maybe Rosie needs someone to help keep track of Harold, you know, keep him on the right path," Jay observed.

"Rosie relies on Jesse to reassurance herself that the boys are not getting into too much mischief." Jay noted the misused word, but he would never correct her.

Sara petted Gatito, her caramel-colored cat stretched out on her lap. "When Jesse travels for his religious duties, Paco often stays with Harold and Rosie Dawn. Neither young man has quite figured out his future. Jesses sometimes goes camping with them in Cougar Canyon for a night or two. I guess he wants them to grow up right."

"How did Jesse get involved with the *cofradía*?"

"Well, I told you, he always helps out with the societies that take care of the poor. He takes food to families who need it. He even gives rides to town to people in that big fancy Cadillac car. He works hard for the people here." She sipped her tea and continued.

"Joshua and I were surprised when Jesse, maybe four years ago, was elected *hermano mayor*. He's the youngest one ever elected from here. He feels very grateful for the confidence that his elders have shown him. He's not an outsider any more, but I don't think he feels secure, maybe because his family left him. He takes his role as leader of the *cofradía* seriously, and he is a devoted father to Paco. But it seems like he always has to show himself off to others." She shifted in the rocking chair to ease her back.

"I don't know if I should say this," paused the gentle lady, her voice dropping to a whisper. "But he does act like a rooster sometimes."

Jay smiled at Sara and she smiled back.

Rumor Mill

Jesse's conversation with Jay to see if he knew anything about the statue's disappearance had convinced him that Jay knew nothing. Thinking about the statue, Jesse recalled the past several years and his involvement as an officer of the *cofradía*. The first meeting of the leaders he attended was held in Rinconcito in 1970. The men had met in a secluded adobe building which, Jesse heard, was one of the *moradas* closed down by the Church in the 1930s. Now, other religious groups used the space for retreats and meetings. He enjoyed the prayers, and he liked discussing ideas about caring for the welfare of the people with other religious leaders from nearby settlements. It was then Jesse first heard rumors that upset him.

It was whispered that the Church was contemplating changes. The diocese owned too many dilapidated buildings it could no longer afford to keep up. The cost of repairs was rising and the settlements were losing people to larger towns. Cutting back on the number of mission chapels could save the diocese money. Since outlying missions seldom had resident priests, the pastors had to travel long distances to celebrate Mass. The pastor was obligated to visit each mission several times during the year to hear confessions, celebrate Mass, hold baptisms and preside at First Communions. The cost to keep vehicles road-worthy enough to travel ill-kept rural routes was substantial. Harsh weather made their upkeep even more expensive. It was said that the Church might have to close some of its mission chapels.

Jesse had become concerned about these rumors. When he asked the older men at a meeting, they pooh-poohed the idea and dismissed it as "just talk." Jesse believed the older men knew much more than he about the workings of the Church, so he resolved not to worry about it.

By lunch time, business had been concluded. The ladies of Rinconcito brought in heavy trays of food. After giving thanks for a good meal and a successful meeting, the *hermanos mayores* of the *cofradías* readied themselves to get home. Refreshed, they prepared to rededicate themselves to care for the needy and sick in their communities. Most of the *heromanos* had miles to travel over back roads, so they scattered to their trucks to load up their belongings and papers. They all wanted to get home before dark.

Jesse had just put on his Dallas Cowboys cap and was about to get into his truck when he saw Miguel, the other younger man in the group. Jesse had spoken with him a few times. He liked Miguel. He'd look forward to seeing him at the next meeting.

When he saw Jesse, Miguel gave a quick turn of his head and pursed his lips, pointing to a nearby grove of trees. Jesse figured he had something on his mind, so he nodded back. Each strolled separately away from the meeting house toward the grove that would screen them from view. Anyone who noticed would assume they were going to take a leak.

"What's on your mind, Miguel?"

Miguel answered in a conspiratorial tone. "Listen, Jesse, I think the old guys here are just avoiding the truth. They don't want to believe that our mission churches could be closed down. You know what? I believe it's going to happen."

"Why do you say that?" Jesse asked with concern.

"Because something happened about ten years ago where I live, over in the next county, up near the lake. It's been a family secret because some people might think bad things about my *tío* Daniel and what he and the priest did. Some might be jealous, so our family was warned to keep it quiet. But I want to tell you. Then you'll know that it could happen. It's a true story but you have to promise me that you won't tell anybody."

Jesse looked at Miguel to indicate he agreed to keep quiet.

"My *tío* Daniel, was much older than my dad," said Miguel. "He died about, maybe, 10 years ago. *Tío* Daniel, he was the *mayordomo* of the church, San Gabriel Arcángel. A few days before he died, *Tío* Daniel told us, for the first time, this story. We were all around his bed. He was propped up on pillows so he could breathe better. This is what he told us."

"You all know," *Tío* Daniel said, "that I was *mayordomo* of our little church. One day I decided to check on the church on my way down the mountain where I'd been cutting wood for the winter. As I rounded the last turn on the uneven, muddy road, I could see the white belfry on top of the tin roof between the pointed treetops. I noticed fresh tire tracks in the mud. When I got closer, I saw a rusty, green Ford truck parked behind the church near a grove of aspens.

"Right away, I knew he was there. I pulled up near the entrance, turned off the engine, and pulled out my cigarette papers and pouch of tobacco. My hands were shaking when I tried to roll my cigarette. I got flakes all over. I just waited.

"When the Irish priest came around the corner, he seemed disoriented. His shoulders slumped, and his face was a mask of tragedy. At that moment, I realized that the rumors we had heard were true.

"'Hey, Father B! What are you doing?' I yelled.

"He looked confused and a bit irritated at the interruption. It must have taken him the whole day to summon the energy to do what he had to do.

"I watched him take out a long latch key and approach the front doors of the church. I couldn't be quiet no more.

"No, Father! Stop! I jumped out of my truck. What are you doing? You can't just lock our church with everything inside and walk away. What will the people here do? Father Brennan lifted his sad, reddened eyes and looked at me. Still, he said nothing."

Tío Daniel coughed but went on. "I was so upset that my voice came out high, like a girl's. I even shouted again at poor Fr. Brennan.

"If nobody takes care of the chapel, the roof will cave in – it already leaks, rain will melt the adobes, all our saints, the Stations, the hand-embroidered altar cloths, the vessels, the vestments – they will all be destroyed. Don't do it, Father! Don't abandon the chapel. Somebody could break in and take all the sacred objects. Then they'll sell our *patrimonio* to people who don't even value them."

"Daniel, my son, I have my orders," Father Brennan told me. "There is no choice. I made a vow of obedience."

"Father Brennan and I stood facing each other, mirroring each other's disbelief. Neither of us spoke for long time. A rumble of thunder echoed along the rim of the canyon. It got louder and then rolled into the next canyon. It was a warning of *el porvenir.* He looked like San Juan at the foot of the cross, *abrumado.*

"I continued to yell at him, God forgive me," my *tío* said. "My family and I will preserve the sacred belongings. I promise we will safeguard them. Since the bishop doesn't seem to care what happens to us, who knows? We might even have to build our own chapel!

"Father Brennan turned toward the door and removed the key from the latch. He shook hands with me. We were both trying not to cry."

"'My son, thank you,'" he said at last to my *tío.* "'I will help you load the big pieces. Then I will turn away. Do what you must. When I hear the sound of your truck leaving, I will lock the church for good, as I was ordered to do."

The priest clenched his fists, and his eyes filled with tears.

"We gave big *abrazos* to each other, like brothers. Then, at exactly the same time, we both exclaimed, '*Dios te bendiga.*'

"So, that's what happened," Miguel continued. "It explained all the things my *tío* had in his house, like old pews, and fancy cloths, and little bottles that hold the wine and the water during Mass. So, that's why I think that it could happen again. I believe you are a man of honor, Jesse. So, now you know. *Es la verdad.*"

"*Ay, que triste. Es como una fábula.* Thanks for telling me. I will keep this sad secret and think more about it. Does anyone else know about this?" asked Jesse.

"Either they don't know, or they don't want to know, I guess," Miguel concluded.

Jesse and Miguel shook hands and headed to their trucks. Thunderheads were forming over the mountains. They needed to get home.

Jesse was overwhelmed by the story Miguel had shared with him. It thundered in his brain in unison with the long rumblings from canyon to canyon he heard on the long drive back to Villa Vieja.

Prayers Pounding Heaven

The tolling of the bell on a weekday meant trouble in Villa Vieja. Had someone died? Did another bear come too close to the village? Was there a fire? It wasn't the season for fires, but lately nothing followed the old routines. Even the weather was unpredictable. Was someone hurt? Was a rescue team being formed? The most benign reason the bell tolled was to alert the people that a church service was about to begin.

As soon as the sound echoed off the limestone cliffs and bounced along following the curves of the river, plans for the day shifted. The villagers straightened their shoulders and readied themselves.

Men in the fields and forests stopped their machines and cleaned their hands; wives wiped the flour from their hands with dish towels, washed their faces, and got the children corralled. The children asked why the bell was ringing. They had faced plenty of challenges before. The villagers made their way to the chapel.

Joshua and Sara arrived before the others and opened the chapel. Joshua looked somber and much older, she thought as she looked at her brother's beloved face.

As the people began to arrive, she smiled and greeted each one. Sara tried to look reassuring. People took their seats in their own pews made by a member of the family and sometimes passed from one generation to the next. The pews were of varying colors, comfort, and stability. Some had kneelers, but most knelt on the wooden floor. Long services demanded sacrifice, especially for the knees.

Sara saw Rosie Dawn and Harold come in. A rumor was circulating that Doña Amarga had refused to share her pew with them even though Mando, her foster son, had brought them to Villa Vieja and deserted them. Rosie Dawn and Harold had built their own pew and painted it light blue. The villagers were impressed with their gumption and skill. She and her son had almost become members of the community. As Sara looked around, there was no one present in the church she did not know.

It was time. Joshua, with Sara at his side, stood in front of the altar, took a deep breath, wheezed a little, and blessed himself with the Sign of the Cross as did all the others, finishing with the gesture of kissing a cross made with the thumb and index finger.

"*Mis hermanos y hermanos,* may God bless us and our task. We are here for a very important reason. As you know, the Santo Niño made by our great-grandfather, Old Mister Benavídez, has been in this church for over one hundred years." He swallowed and continued. "Our valuable patrimony has been cared for by the village over the years. I have sad news. The statue is missing from the place it is always kept."

Gasps were audible, several older women began to cry softly and one loud wail reminded everyone of *La Llorona* searching for her children. People looked at each other with puzzled concern.

"So, I beg of you, has anyone any information about the little statue? Do you know where it is? Did someone borrow it and not tell Filomeno, or my sister and me?" He paused and looked around the chapel, his kindly, sad eyes twin mirrors brimming with hope and pain.

The church was silent.

Joshua spoke again. "I hear nothing that makes me think the statue is safe. Therefore, we will begin this evening to pray a novena to the Santo Niño. We will pray for the intercession of His Mother, the Blessed Virgin Mary, to help us find it.

"I do not have to tell you all that this is a great disgrace – for the culprits and for us. Pray that the statue of the Holy Child will be found whole and safely returned to us. You can help. Try to think. Have you noticed anything suspicious or unusual that might lead us to the happy conclusion of finding our statue? If you have any information, you may come to any member of the team – me, my sister, Jesse, Ernie, Doña Amargarita or Rosie."

At this, many heads turned to look at Rosie with surprise. "And Jay, our favorite son, is here to help us." Joshua looked at Jay and smiled.

"Remember, any information you give us will be kept in total confidence as we go forth.

"Ask the *santero*, old Mr. Benavídez, too, to intercede for us in Heaven that we may find his statue. Again, does anyone wish to say something?"

A few seconds passed. The sounds of shuffling feet, the scrape of boots, and the creaking of the pews gave no answers. Joshua bowed his head.

Not wanting to lose an opportunity for recognition, Jesse stood up.

"As you know, I am the *hermano mayor* of the *cofradía*," he said. "May Villa Vieja be protected from evil and may this unfortunate event not cause dissention, but bring us to harmony and peace. Amen. Don't forget. We will meet here again tonight to start the novena."

A few amens could be heard as the villagers filed out the heavy doors into a day that had darkened and grown somber. An enormous cloud seemed to hover above the tiny community. They returned to their tasks slowly, carrying a new cross of sadness.

For the next nine weeks, the faithful of Villa Vieja would gather in the chapel to pray the *Novena Dedicated to the Most Miraculous Child of Atocha* for the return of the Santo Niño, their very own saint. As they departed, they wished each other a good night.

"*Hasta mañana.*"
"*Vaya con Dios.*"

It was mid-October when the novena began. Villagers hoped the cold had not come to stay. Winter tested one's endurance in the high valley. Families had harvested their crops and stacked high piles of pine and juniper firewood under the eaves for winter. Russet leaves that had blazed saffron and gold in early autumn were swirled into crunchy piles that turned sodden and dark. Sudden gusts of wind blew off hats and chilled ears and noses. Naked branches of bare trees reminded everyone how the hard winters in Villa Vieja challenged one's spirits. Slippery roads. Clayey mud trapped vehicles up to their hubcaps. Pipes froze. People got sick. The gas company trucks did not come when promised due to icy curves. Sometimes the drifts were so high that all were snowed in. Even the large yellow school bus could not get to Frontera, much to the delight of the children who played in the snow and then warmed and dried themselves next to wood stoves in the cozy kitchens filled with aromas of beans and chile simmering on the stove.

Most villagers were horrified by the disappearance of the Niño. It seemed too big a crime, too serious a sin for such a small place. A climate of unease descended on the roofs like snow clouds on the dark evergreen forests. Could it be someone in Villa Vieja who had taken it? Neighbors looked out of the corners of their eyes and speculated. Old hurts festered and were amplified by gossip. If anyone left the village without mentioning where they were going, others would suspect the worst.

Praying a novena was a tradition. The readings and prayers occurred in sets of nine days or nine weeks and could be individual or communal. The format of the Santo Niño's novena alternated readings in the centuries-old elaborated style of expressive language common in Spanish with simple verses and familiar prayers, many known by heart. Those who were not literate in Spanish could still participate. The *rezador* led the formal prayers and the people responded with singing and repetitive responses. The 19th century archaic Spanish expressed a sense of an intimate familiarity with the saints and awe of the power of God in people's lives. Extravagant praise of both the Child and the Mother flowed through the orations in great detail, clothed in glorious, poetic language. The eloquence of the language transported listeners to glorious heights far above their daily experiences.

Joshua cracked his knuckles and signaled for quiet. Being a descendant of Old Mister Benavídez lent gravity and an edge of sorrow to the *rezador*'s voice when he spoke of these perplexing events. Sounds of light coughing, babies whimpering, and the creaking of the old kneelers began to die down.

The First Night's prayers began with an Act of Contrition addressed to the "Most Handsome Child of Atocha." All present asked pardon for their transgressions, for mercy, and for the success of their petitions. Next, they beseeched Mary, the Most Holy Mother, to intercede for them asking her to "turn toward me your most beautiful eyes... enlighten this darkened and wretched soul... so antiquated and moth-eaten... renew it, restore it to its original grace, grant what I ask on this day and request it for me from your Son, Jesus."

Each night had a rigid and specific structure of prayer and response. The First Appeal followed. Its simplicity contrasted dramatically with the embellished Spanish used elsewhere:

> "Little Child of Atocha,
> amazing little Child,
> divine little Child,
> kneeling we ask
> like a powerful One:
> may my afflictions
> return to me as joy
> for you are my Father,
> my delight and my tranquility."

Next, miracles attributed to the Child and His Mother were recounted. On the first night, they listened to the First Miracle followed by the First Day Prayer, the Proposal of the Request, and a series of the familiar prayers, Our Fathers, Hail Marys, and Glorias.

The First Day Prayer extolled the overarching theme of the entire novena which honors the intimate connection between the Holy Child and mother Mary's womb, the container that brought the Son of God to earth, is glorified. Her womb creates a frame around concentric circles of narrative which present various scenes from the Bible, references to events in the life of Christ, mentioned other great saints, gave accounts of miracles attributed to the Holy Child, and cited various apparitions of the Holy Child and His Mother. At the center of this vision, the Child is held up in apotheosis to radiate His love to the world. The Holy Mother appears as advocate and mediator, and most of all, a human mother. The grace of God comes through her as Jesus Christ came through her.

When the lengthy first evening's prayers ended, people got up stiffly. Knees cracked. Backs creaked. The faithful offered up their pain so that their little statue would be safely returned. Tired and pensive, families climbed into pickups and headed to the warmth of home. The small children were all asleep and had to be carried. Those who lived close by walked into the chill. The prayers reminded the people of Villa Vieja of the links between this world and the next, their own sinfulness, the presence of evil, and the love that could save them. Subdued voices of those who had walked to the chapel could be heard under a dark sky with scant stars.

"What a shame."

"It's terrible. I wonder who did such an ugly thing."

"What is this world coming to?"

"Let's hope the *Niñito* is not damaged."

"Ojalá we find out who did this soon."

"Ojalá que sí. I hope so."

"Hasta mañana."

"Vaya con Dios."

Life in Villa Vieja went off kilter. Unease affected everyone. As the weeks went by with no leads, the people began to suspect that the statue had disappeared for good. Had it been sold? Was it damaged, or hidden away somewhere for some perverse reason? The villagers had always enjoyed the care of the Santo Niño hovering around them like a cloak. Now they felt vulnerable and unsafe. Nerves were strung tight. They feared that God had abandoned them. How could they gain back His care? Many lit candles and recited extra prayers, convinced that God was punishing them for not continuing their traditions.

A few days after the novena began, an old auntie swore that she had seen the *Niño* walking down the road with sandals on his feet. He was wearing a cowboy hat with a chicken feather stuck in the crown. No one believed her. She was *loca.*

During the first week of the novena, Mrs. Mondragón accused Mrs.Pino of leaving her gate open so that her goats got out and damaged her house plants on the front porch. Mrs. Pino refused to apologize. Mrs. Mondragón put a big stick on her front porch.

The next week, unusually high winds blew down two barns and an old outhouse. Two people in the village complained of food poisoning. Doña Amarga treated them but wondered why their vomiting would not stop.

During the third week a fistfight broke out after Mass when Mr. Flores suggested that Mr. Montoya's mother was so forgetful that she probably took the statute and forgot where she put it. Mr. Montoya punched Mr. Flores in the stomach. He laughed and replied, "Just kidding."

By week four, Mando had disappeared again without notice. Someone started a rumor that Rosie was pregnant. Paco's girlfriend broke up with him because he was spending too much time with Harold.

The fifth week, a falling-down log cabin burned to the ground. Someone accused Harold and Paco of starting it. When Mrs. Otero dreamed that a long-haired man with a moustache carried the statue away under his arm and headed south for Mexico, everyone looked suspiciously at anyone with long hair.

The following week, a branch of an old cottonwood collapsed the roof of Mr. Ruiz's flimsy barn and knocked out his best milk cow. She stopped giving milk.

In November, rumors spread that Jesse had accused Sara and Joshua out of jealousy of the *mayordomos.* Joshua and Sara stopped speaking to him.

On December 11, the ladies arrived to clean the chapel and to decorate it for the Feast of Our Lady of Guadalupe. Everyone acted wary and suspicious of everyone else.

"Who do you think took it?"

"I'll bet it's that old grouch, Mr. Flores. He don't like the church no more."

"Well, I think it was one of those hippies up in Rocky Point. They take everything they find and try to sell it. "

"Maybe Ernie is in on it. You know how the *policia* is. You can't trust nobody no more."

"At least we have the fiesta of Our Lady to be glad about."

Black Habits

Father Xavier Toledo (Fr. X) slumped in a chair too large for him in the parish office of St. Cecilia's, a struggling, run-down parish in Frontera. His eyes, too close to his ferret-like nose, narrowed as he pondered the piles of correspondence and too-high stack of bills that teetered on the crude desk with one leg shorter than the other three. Black strands of hair covered an incipient bald spot on his elongated skull. Down-turned lips gave him a wary expression. A vein pulsed in his left temple. His jaws chewed the gum in his mouth like a crushing machine.

Due to a dramatic decline in vocations several years before, the area's bishop, Bishop Kenney, had been in need of priests. Strongly Hispanic Catholic families no longer urged at least one son to devote his life to God, as in the past. New opportunities were opening up – better jobs, access to more education, increased prosperity. The bishop, with reluctance, had put in a request for the loan of priests from other dioceses several years before.

A few weeks later one candidate, a skinny little man, arrived at the Chancery Office to volunteer. When Bishop Kenney met Fr. X, he was pleased to learn that he spoke Spanish, although with an unfamiliar accent. Even the bishop was put off by Fr. X's imperious manner. They spoke briefly. After he left, the bishop sighed. Well, God writes straight with crooked lines. This instrument is going to need a lot of straightening and sharpening. But, he reminded himself, it was God's will that Fr. X was here, and some good would surely come of his presence. But the bishop couldn't quite see how.

For several years, Fr. X had worked in the Chancery Office, the headquarters of the diocese. His success had seemed assured. He rubbed cassocks with the bishop on a daily basis. His calculated goal was to rise in the ranks of the hierarchy to a position of power to which he knew he belonged by virtue of his education and intelligence.

When Bishop Kenney decided to send Fr. X to St. Cecilia's to fill in for the aged and beloved pastor, Padre Pedroso, who could no longer celebrate Mass because of unsteadiness of feet and fogginess of mind, Fr. X resented what he considered a demotion.

And now, this pathetic little parish. Dissatisfied, the petulant *padre* chafed at his loss of status like a child picking a scab. If he had wanted to be ministering to every whim of simple and poorly-educated parishioners, he would have chosen to be a pastor. After the sacrifices he had made to come to this place, so bereft of culture, Fr. X thought he deserved more. The parish reminded him of the dusty village in Castile where he had grown up. He had chosen to be a priest because it offered him a way out of poverty, not because it offered a road to Heaven. Ordained in Spain, he had had one moment of generosity when he asked to be assigned to work in the southwest United States as a missionary to the Indians. He loved books about the Wild West and was a virtual scholar on the Indian Wars. Fr. X was unaware that he would encounter in the Southwest worse deprivation and isolation than he had ever seen in Spain. And now, he was asked to work with descendants of Spanish émigrés from medieval Spain. What a comedown.

Fr. X had one great gift, of which he was very proud, his eloquence as a preacher. Even his detractors had to admit that he was a masterly performer. He could raise people's emotions from fear to anger and to shame at will. Fr. X sensed the power he had over others. In the exhortatory style of a traveling evangelist, with wave upon wave of words that built, crested, and broke, he brought people to their knees. The detritus of their self-esteem melted into the sands of guilt. He ranted at sinners, castigating them for having offended God. He cited chapter and verse of the Scriptures with precision.

Fr. X lost the essence of the Word in his flights of imagination and fury. Like the early Pilgrim preacher, Jonathan Edwards, he spewed fire and brimstone, no hint of sweet salvation. The "man of God" got so carried away that he jumped up and down as he tongue-lashed his flock into submission. Prancing in front of the altar, his decibels could shake dust from the rafters. It was reported that he actually foamed at the mouth, spitting saliva on those unlucky members of the congregation seated in the front pews.

The reception at St. Cecilia's had been cool and guarded. Missing their beloved Padre Pedroso, the parishioners would have been skeptical of any new priest. However, with traditional Hispanic hospitality, they offered the replacement priest their respect and introduced themselves. The minute Fr. X opened his mouth, they wondered at his Spanish. A few had to force themselves not to laugh at the Spanish from Spain that exited his lips. His accent made it hard for these northern New Mexicans to understand what he said. Their own Rio Arriba dialect was good enough for them.

Fr. X started by laying down strict rules by which he would govern the parish, knowing nothing of its history. Many of the families who frequented the sturdy church, built of squared bluff sandstone, had ancestry that went back over four hundred years. Their *antepasados* were buried in the church yard. Their families had kept the church operative for generations without much guidance from the few priests who came and went. It was they who knew how to hold the community together through faith and mutual support.

When religious leaders invited Fr. X to a meeting to introduce the leaders of the parish organizations – the sodality, the altar society, the *cofradía*, and numerous other committees – Fr. X hid his yawns behind his thin, manicured hands. He shifted his body in his seat and glanced out the windows. He was unimpressed. After all, he was ordained. He had theological training and a classical education. Nothing they could say would deter him from his conviction that Europeans were superior to the New World natives. He believed that the *raza* had degraded in the broiling sun of the desert southwest.

Fr. X would make them obey, so that St. Cecilia's would become a model parish. Besides, didn't he have the bishop on his side? He would impress the bishop with his zeal. In not too long, he would be back in the Chancery Office. He licked his lips in satisfaction.

Fr. X looked around the dingy office. Through a small window on the left, he could see the magnificence of the mountains.

On the right, he saw the barrenness of the plains. Fr. X knew exactly on which side he belonged.

The sharp ring of the rotary dial phone broke his concentration.

"Fr. Toledo here. Who's calling?"

A low voice murmured something.

"Speak up! I can't hear you."

"Father, I have some news that you should know. I want to meet with you. Where nobody, *nadie*, can see us."

"Who are you? Identify yourself."

"I'm from Villa Vieja. There are things going on at the little chapel you should know about."

Fr. X dimly recalled that name. It was one of the pesky small mission chapels for which he was responsible. He had not yet visited any of them.

"How do I know this is not a trick? What's going on? Why should I believe you?"

"Because I tell the truth. There are strange happenings in the village up there. I think you should know about them."

The padre had to think carefully about his response. At least the caller seemed to respect him and the church. No one else had shown him any consideration.

"What do you suggest?"

"Meet me at the restaurant near the Y intersection in Frontera near the old Safeway. Go on Monday evening. Nobody goes there on Mondays. Sit way in the back. Wait until after dark, about eight o'clock. Wear civvies. No collar."

"How will I know you?"

"I'll be wearing a faded denim jacket with silver buttons and a big turquoise ring on my right hand. I'll be way in the back."

Somewhat intrigued, the padre retorted, "Be there on time."

"I will. *Hasta la vista, padre.*"

Fr. X disliked going out in the evening. An unexpected snowfall had dumped heavy, wet snow on the town. Fewer people would be out. He shoved armloads of snow off the windshield of the '59 Chevy that belonged to the parish and started the engine. His drive to the restaurant yielded only a couple of slow, sliding moments. When he saw the Y intersection, he turned left into a small shopping area. He saw a shoe repair shop, a meat market, and a dark-fronted liquor store. At the north end of the parking lot, an "Open" sign blinked in red neon. The priest parked in front of the meat market away from the entrance to the restaurant. He slogged through the snow toward the sign. Through its dingy window, he saw a dog-eared menu curved behind the glass listing the restaurant's ordinary fare.

Fr. X entered the restaurant in plain clothes, hatless. He wore a grey sweatshirt with no logos, tan pants, an overcoat three sizes too large for him, and a thick, pilled wool scarf around his neck. He had found a pair of old loafers, probably Padre Pedroso's, in the closet at the rectory. They fit, but low shoes were not a good choice for an evening of cold and snow. His feet were chilled. Discomfort did not improve his mood. He hoped the restaurant would be warm. In the vestibule, he chewed the inside of his cheek and waited to be seated. When the hostess greeted him, he jumped.

"Good evening, sir. Where would you like to sit?" asked the pony-tailed waitress.

"In the back. I'm meeting a client."

As the teenager guided him toward the back, the priest noticed a few scattered customers. Most seemed to be laborers tired after long hours. The men ate quickly, intent on the food. He heard no conversation.

"I think your client is already here." She led him to the back, her ponytail bouncing with each step.

She showed him to the table. The rather tall person seated there wore a faded denim blue jacket with silver buttons and a large turquoise ring. The padre sighed. They did not shake hands.

"You arrived early."

"I am glad you came." They eyed each other like circling dogs.

"What is it you have to tell me?" inquired the priest in his abrupt manner.

"Oh, Father, let's order first. Food makes the message taste better."

Both ordered regular coffee and *posole* for a cold evening. Neither could resist apple pie à la mode, heated, of course. The perky waitress brought the orders, left the check on the table between them. She went back to the kitchen to chat with cook in her chirpy voice about Saturday's football win and her cheerleading doings.

"Tell me why you are here," demanded Fr.X.

"Well, you're new here, Father. Let me give you a little background. The carving of the Santo Niño de Atocha is very important to Villa Vieja. It was carved over one hundred years ago by a famous *santero* from Escondido whose descendants still live in the village." The informant swallowed a sip of coffee. He looked the priest straight in the eye.

"The statue has vanished from the chapel."

"Why has no one told me of this?" Fr. X could feel the pulse twitching in his temple. "Why didn't anyone let the pastor know?"

"We all know Padre Pedroso is not himself any more. Besides, the disappearance is a big disgrace for the people. They are very upset and don't want to tell the Church. They feel ashamed."

"But the mission chapels are under my jurisdiction now." The thought that this would make him look bad with the bishop flashed through Fr. X's mind. He had not wanted to visit all the missions. They were spread out all over, and he hated to drive.

"How long ago did this happen?" he asked.

"Uh, almost two months ago, Father."

"How dare they not tell me? Who do you think is behind this – the secrecy, not the disappearance itself?"

"The *mayordomos*, Joshua and Sara – brother and sister – are getting old and forgetful. I don't know if they can handle taking care of the chapel any more. Maybe they have something to do with it. *¿Quién sabe?*"

Fr. X felt a burning rash begin to spread up his chest and onto his face. His mouth was so dry that his tongue stuck to the roof of it. He half-lifted his small body from the seat and leaned into the face of the informant. He tried to control his voice, low with rage.

"I will report this atrocity to the bishop," waggling his finger back and forth, "but first, I want you to swear to support me. I will go right away to Villa Vieja. They should be ashamed of themselves for, for, for insubordination! That's what it is, and I won't have this arrogant behavior, taking church ma, ma, matters into their own hands. *Qué verguënza.*"

"*Padre*, the last week of the novena is tomorrow night. There is time. You must contact Joshua and Sara tonight. Tomorrow evening, everyone will be at the chapel."

Fr. X considered this idea for a moment.

"Can you pick me up yourself? I don't even know where Villa Vieja is." He hated to drive, especially on unknown roads.

The informant's raised eyebrows and offended expression made no impression on the priest. Father X was unaware of the deep pride the people had in their hamlets.

"Oh, no, Father, I can't do that. Everyone would figure out that I had spoken to you. You have to support me, too. Keep this quiet. Please call the *mayordomos* tonight – it's not too late. Set up an appointment for tomorrow afternoon. Tell them you have information from the bishop. They can't say no."

"They won't get away with this *desgracia*. I'll put a stop to this flaunting of the authority of the Church." Fr. X's eyes were barely visible, his whole face flushed and squinched tight, as though he had bitten into a raw tamarind fruit. "I'll do what you suggest."

"I have given you important information. There is something you can do to repay me."

"Are you demanding some kind of reward from me? *¡Qué Satanás!*" fumed the priest.

"Oh no, *Padre*. I just want a promise that you will withdraw any support for Joshua and Sara in the next election. Tell them, well, order them, not to seek re-election as *mayordomos*. They are getting too old to protect the chapel. There are others who want to serve."

"I'll take your request under consideration."

"Make the calls tonight while there is still time," urged the informant.

The wary allies shook hands. The informant left for the dark drive back to Villa Vieja.

Fr. X hefted the heavy, damp overcoat from the back of the chair and made a quick stop in the men's room before he left. He felt a shiver even before he stepped through the exit beneath the blinking neon sign. Fr. X stomped through the light snow in his borrowed loafers only to find the Chevy's windshield coated with a frosty glaze.

Return of the Santo

An unexpected storm in mid-October left a thin crust of snow that turned the valley into a white expanse punctuated with evergreen limbs decked out with icicles hanging from their branches. All day long animals and humans had snuggled down into whatever warmth they could find. The snow, like cotton batting, absorbed and muted the normal sounds of the season – no crows cawing, no chainsaw whining, no rumble of a pickup loaded with wood grinding its gears on the way to town. The valley and its inhabitants took advantage of the lull and enjoyed a winter siesta, grateful for a legitimate reason to rest from their labors. Smoke rose from houses in pale oblongs resembling calla lilies, twisting slowly against the dark grey sky. By 6:30 in the evening, everything was dark and settled for the night. Even the dogs were allowed inside sheds or houses due to the cold. Deer nestled under low brush, nuzzling the snow melting with their warm breath for a bit of moisture. Bears, unaware, remained ensconced in caves high on the mountain for winter. The mischievous coyotes lay low.

No one knew yet what had happened in the chill of the night before.

From high in Cougar Canyon, two bulky figures, heavily bundled against the cold, had descended toward the village. A disinterested turkey vulture perched unseen in a dark tree. They made their way carefully down the trail. Snow masked the loose rocks and the trail's steep drop-off. Neither spoke. Occasionally, one or the other lit a small flashlight to guide their way. Although they had planned their mission for weeks, they had not considered the arrival of an early snow. No use talking about it now. They had to complete their task tonight or else. Neither dared consider the consequences if they were discovered. When they got close to the village, they whispered.

"What if somebody sees us? What if somebody's there?" asked the shorter one, feeling his fear grow like an icy snowball in his gut.

"You *burro*! Why would anyone be at the church now? Don't worry," scoffed the other.

The back door had a new lock. They approached the back of the building and found the door was unlocked. Surprised, they let themselves into the sacristy.

"Do you still have the flashlight?"

"Of course. I'm not stupid," was the retort. No, not stupid, but afraid, yes, but not about to admit it.

The door from the sacristy into the chapel was closed. So far, so good. They took the bag from the backpack with great care and rested it in the spot where the priest always stood to vest himself for services. They wanted to sneak an admiring peek at the piece, but did not. For a moment, they wondered if what they were doing was a sin. They looked at each other and winked. Audacity mixed with guilt and trepidation made their adrenaline surge. No one will ever find out, they both thought with satisfaction. The taller one pushed open the door to the sanctuary. The other carried the small bag like a mother with a newborn. They faced the rear of the altarpiece.

"Just put it where it goes, and let's get out of here!"

As the shorter one started to put the bag into its accustomed space under the altar, they both heard a cough. They flinched and nearly wet themselves. Waves of panic shot through them. The taller one ran toward the sound.

Near the old gas stove, a figure rose up slowly and said, "Who's there?"

In the dim light, Filomeno's rheumy eyes strained to see who had entered the chapel. When the opaque eyes found their focus, recognition, then anguish, filled them. He recognized the taller one. Sick with guilt, the intruder pushed hard against Filomeno to escape the disillusionment reflected in those eyes. He fell with a loud thump and lay still.

"Let's get the hell out of here!" shouted the shorter one. They heard groaning as they slammed the back door of the chapel and ran toward the river. They ran in the cold night until exhausted. They crept into an old barn and hid there until dawn, afraid to go home. The shorter one tossed the empty pack behind two boulders on the north bank of the river.

As quickly as the storm had come, it left the canyon. A glorious sun shone in a cloudless sky the next morning, and by ten o'clock, there were only traces of snow left in the shadows.

Sara had arrived at the chapel early to meet the Altar Society ladies to clean the chapel for the celebration feast of Our Lady of Guadalupe the next day. When she opened the large front door, Sara saw a crumpled heap near the back kneeler. Below it, a reddish brown ooze outlined the head of a prone figure on the light blue floor.

"*Ay, Dios mío!*" she exclaimed as she recognized the body of Filomeno. He had stopped by last night to tell Joshua that he was going to the chapel to check the stove for leaks. Sara timidly approached and knelt beside him. His white hair was pinkish red with blood. She called to him in a soft voice, "Filomeno, can you hear me?" There was no answer. She cradled the head of their old friend in her arms.

"What happened?" Doña Amargarita asked with surprising calm when she saw Filomeno and the blood. Of course, she was used to dealing with emergencies.

"I think he must have tripped on a loose floor board and hit his head on one of the pews," Sara said.

"Go get Joshua," Sara continued. "Find Jesse. Tell him to bring his big car. Hurry! They'll have to drive Filomeno to town to the hospital."

"*Bueno, me voy.* I'll tell Joshua and Jesse. I need to get my bag of *remedios* from home. Oh, here comes your niece, Gracia. Let her get them. I'll go straight to my house."

The old *curandera* headed out and swung her ample body from side to side as she lumbered toward her house near the river.

Sara supported Filomeno's head in her lap until Doña Amargarita returned with her bag.

The *curandera* washed Filomeno's head wounds with water infused with herbs and chanted over him. When she used her healing gifts, she went into what some would call a trance. She seemed removed from her surroundings to a place of spiritual beings. She was intoning a chant over the wounded sacristan when Jesse and Joshua arrived to take him to the hospital in Frontera.

Doña Amarga feared the worst as she watched Sara climb into the car after the men, saying her rosary. She had done the best she could. Now Filomeno's life was in the hands of the doctors, and God.

First the disappearance of the little saint and now this. What was happening to the community of Villa Vieja, wondered La Doña as she lumbered home. *¡Qué vergüenza!* What a shame upon the village. Who had done this and why? Even she, who usually heard all the rumors and stories before anyone else, was surprised. She would have to keep her ears open. She wondered if she were losing some of her powers.

Soon the ladies began arriving. Since Sara had decided to go in the car to the hospital with Filomeno, Doña Amarga had to explain to each one what had occurred.

"How badly is Filomeno hurt?"

"He was unconscious. There was dried blood, a lot, all around his head. I tried to get him to talk, but no luck. I cleaned him a little and said some special prayers. I did everything I could."

"Who took him to town?"

"Joshua, Sara and Jesse. Now let's get to work."

Before they began to clean, the ladies knelt and asked God not to take the dear old man. Everyone was shocked.

The news of Filomeno's injury spread through the village like a forest fire. Neighbors ran to tell the others, and telephone lines hummed with activity. The sense of unease that had been building changed into certainty. God was upset with the village. First the theft and now an assault. What was happening in this "vale of tears?"

Cleaning the chapel took longer than usual. Friends whispered to each other lamenting the accident. The women were anxious about Filomeno and their conversation slowed the pace of their cleaning. Mrs. Mondragón got some Lysol from home to clean the blood stains from the floor. Imagine if they had to see the discoloration on the floor every time they came to church! Three of the women scrubbed diligently near the stove. Mrs. Acosta swept the steps of the podium that supported the altar.

Mrs. Durán's job was to clean the altar itself. She cleaned the wax from the candlesticks and dusted each statue. When she went to the sacristy to get clean linens for the altar, she noticed the back door was ajar. She didn't think much about it. Finding the smooth ironed altar cloths in a cabinet, she returned to place them on the altar. When she started toward the back, she glanced ruefully at the space where the Niño had been stored. *¡Qué cosa!* What in Heaven's name? There was something stuffed into the space beside the altar.

"Come see, come here," she exclaimed in a shaking voice. Most of the other women dropped their cleaning cloths and mops to gather around her.

"Look," she said. "There's something in there. See?" The women peered into the shadowy space.

Doña Amargarita took charge, pushing her imposing frame to the front.

"What in the world!" she exclaimed. *"¿Qué es esto?"*

She pulled out a khaki bag.

"Don't you think we should wait to open it until Joshua, Sara and Jesse come back?" ventured Mrs. Mondragón who was so nervous she was twisting her cleaning rags in her hands.

"Why? We don't know what it is. I am not afraid to open it," declared Doña Amarga. "It might be a bunch of garbage. Who knows?"

La Doña placed the bag on the altar platform and plopped herself down. The other women looked on with anxious curiosity. No coughing. No whispers. They could hear the faint gurgle of water as it moved beneath the icy ledges on the river banks.

The *curandera* picked up the bag and turned it from side to side, like a specially wrapped birthday gift. As she lowered it to the platform, the ladies held their collective breath when she reached in and removed a small wooden box wrapped in a blanket.

The box was latched with a leather thong. Doña Amarga untied it with care. The ladies leaned forward as she opened the door. There was the Santo Niño resting on a soft deerskin lining. There it was, as lovable as ever! The Santo Niño looked even better than they remembered. Tears of joy ran down their cheeks. Even the old *curandera* wiped her eyes.

Their statue had returned to them, *gracias a Dios.*

Everyone agreed that the *Niñito* should be left unwrapped on the altar for all to see. They placed it there reverently. Praises and thanksgiving rose from every throat as they looked with love upon their special saint. The ladies organized themselves. Volunteers promised to stand guard in the chapel until the *mayerdomos* returned.

Much later that evening, after the fiesta for Our Lady of Guadalupe had begun, Joshua, Jesse, and Sara returned from the hospital and learned that the statue was back in the chapel. Joshua and Sara were elated at first, but the more they thought about it, *lo más enojados,* the more they became concerned that Doña Amargarita had not waited for them. Jesse, however, was silently pleased that the *mayordomos* had not been consulted first. Maybe their power was waning. His secret desire was to be selected for that honor.

"How is Filomeno? Is he going to be OK?" asked Mrs. Baca.

Jesse, seeing an opportunity to put himself forward, took control of the conversation.

"*Ay, que lástima. Desafortunadamente,* Filomeno is in a coma. He received a hard blow to his head. He might have bleeding into the brain."

"*Jesús, María, y José.*"

"*Qué lástima.*"

"*Ay, pobrecito.*"

Jesse continued. "I talked to the doctors myself. They don't know how long until Filomeno comes out of the coma, if ever. His condition is serious, but they say he is not in imminent danger of death. Pray for him, and be glad our little Santo Niño is back with us. Enjoy the fiesta."

Jesse looked drawn, his long face even more serious than usual.

Little by little, a few began to realize the possibility that Filomeno had not just tripped and fallen. He must have surprised the culprits.

Who and what had Filomeno seen?
What a day of contradictions!

Call from on High

The phone rang in the rectory. Marina, the housekeeper, hurried to answer it. "St. Cecilia's Parish. May we help you?"

"This is Bishop Kenney. I need to speak with Father Toledo."

"Oh, yes, your uh, uh, honor, er, Your Holiness," she stammered. "I'll get Father Xavier right away."

Wide-eyed, she handed the black receiver to Fr. X who was finishing his second cup of coffee. He motioned her into the kitchen and cleared his throat.

"Your Excellency, how are you? It's an honor to hear your voice."

"Fine, thanks. I'll get right to the point, Father Toledo. What's this I hear about the disappearance of the little Santo Niño from the chapel in Villa Vieja? Do you know about this?"

"Well, I can assure Your Excellency, first of all, that there is nothing to worry about. I paid a visit just yesterday to the *mayordomos,* Joshua and Sara. Miraculously, *gracias a Diós*, the statue has been returned to the *capilla*. I scolded them about their laxity and their dishonesty. It seems the intruders entered the chapel with a key. No windows or doors were broken."

"How can you or anyone be sure that it is the real statue that was carved by Old Mister Benavídez?" asked the Bishop. "That statue is a treasure and a legacy to the community. It's over one hundred years old." Then he asked the question that Fr. X had dreaded.

"When did you learn of this shameful occurrence?"

Fr. X could not lie to the bishop who, no doubt, would surely find out about the novena and his failure to visit the village.

"It, it, I had, uh, just recently, Your Excellency. I am told the people of Villa Vieja tried to keep its disappearance a secret. They did not wish the hierarchy to know about it," he stammered.

"Apparently it was taken two months ago, Father," replied the Bishop. "I want to meet with you in my office next week to discuss your conduct in this matter. My secretary will advise you of the date and time. Examine your conscience carefully about this matter before then."

"Of course, Your Excellency." Fr. X was chagrined.

Again, the Bishop asked, "How do you know it's the real statue?" Fr. X did not answer.

There was a long silence before the bishop continued.

"This is an embarrassment to the church. In order to avoid any further complications, I want the statue's authenticity verified by two experts, Dr. Parkhurst at Frontera University and Señor C. Corazón Corrido, one of our best *santeros*.

"You are in charge of organizing the verification process," he ordered. "Contact Dr. Sheldon Parkhurst at the university. He is a specialist in Southwestern religious art. Have him prepare a list of all the gallery owners and dealers in the area. Have him find out if they have been contacted by anyone wanting to sell a *bulto* of the Santo Niño.

"Next, call Señor C. Corazón Corrido. Everyone calls him 'Corey,' by the way. He is a *santero* and, furthermore, an expert on the history of New Mexico folk art. He uses traditional techniques to make his images. Set up a meeting with them to verify the statue's authenticity within the next two weeks."

"But, sir," Fr. X objected, "the statue has been returned. Everything is back in order in Villa Vieja – Your Highness – oops, Your Excellency. You need not trouble yourself further. I will handle it."

"Think carefully about this matter and do as I said. Go in peace. I will see you soon."

"Yes, Your Excellency."

Fr. X hung up the phone trying to keep his composure. He willed the throbbing in his temple to stop. His thin stomach contracted. Nausea made his mouth water. He was drooling. He licked his lips. He feared that the bishop would never consider him for a higher position now. He saw Marina peek around the door to the kitchen. He stalked out of the dining room and went straight to the office.

The *padre* needed privacy. Dreams for his future were cracking into shards. As he sulked down the dark hallway, he realized that one huge fact had been left out of the conversation. Filomeno, the sacristan, was in a coma fighting for his life. He wondered if the bishop knew. He certainly was not going to be the carrier of any more bad news.

Fr. X located the phone amid the mess on the pastor's desk. He first called Dr. Parkhurst who had just returned from doing laps in the university pool. Parkhurst liked to stay fit, and the locker room was a good place to show off his physique. He believed he was in better shape than most of the students. Fr. X relayed the request for Parkhurst's participation as a consultant in the authentication of the returned Santo Niño.

"I see no reason why not. It is my area of expertise. I'll be glad to be of help," agreed Parkhurst. The good doctor smiled as he contemplated the nice little article he could write about the event later for one of the academic journals to which he subscribed. The more publications that had his name on them the better.

"As soon as I speak with C. Cruz Corrido, I will set up the meeting, with the bishop's approval, of course."

"Oh, I know Corey quite well. We have worked together as consultants on other matters. Would you like for me to call him?"

"No, I believe I should relay the bishop's request myself, thank you. The bishop wants the evaluation to happen as soon as possible. I will call you with the possible dates."

"I understand. I will check my calendar. Christmas break is almost here."

Corey was in his studio when he answered the phone he finally located hidden behind a hunk of half-carved cottonwood root.

"This is Corey."

"This is Father Xavier Toledo, acting pastor at St. Cecilia's. You don't know me yet, but I have been selected by the bishop to contact you. A very strange sequence of events has occurred in Villa Vieja. Have you heard about the disappearance of the old Santo Niño from the chapel there?"

"The one carved by Old Mister Benavídez? No. This is the first I've heard of it. Do they know what happened to it?" Corey perceived reluctance in Fr. X's voice to explain further.

"Miraculously, it was returned, found hidden behind the altar on the morning of December 11. The ladies found it when they were cleaning for the feast of Our Lady of Guadalupe. The bishop would like for you to help authenticate it."

"Of course. I would be glad to see that venerable piece again. It's one of my favorites. When shall we meet? I would prefer after Christmas."

"The bishop wants this to happen right away."

"Well, *Las Posadas* will begin soon, on December 16th. How about the 15th of December in the village? We could meet at the old schoolhouse. I'll need table space and I'll bring some materials as well as reference books, too. Who will be there?"

"I, myself, the *mayordomos*, Sara and Joshua, Jesse, head of the brotherhood, Ernie, Dr. Sheldon Parkhurst, and someone named Jay."

"I know them all. What about Filomeno, the sacristan?"

"Oh, sadly, he was injured by whoever returned the statue. He's still in a coma in the hospital in Frontera."

"*¡Qué lástima!* He's a wonderful old man. I hope he comes to."

"Only God knows whether he will recover," agreed Fr. X in a sanctimonious tone. "So, December 15th at ten o'clock at the old schoolhouse. I will advise the others and report to the bishop."

"I'll call 'Sparky' myself. I haven't talked to him in a while," said Corey.

Fr. Toledo was taken aback by this informality. "I have conveyed the bishop's wishes to Professor Parkhurst already. But, thank you."

After he hung up, Fr. X smirked at another example of lack of good manners he noted in the area. No one would call a college professor by a nickname in Spain.

Altar Egos

The meeting to validate the authenticity of the returned Santo Niño de Atocha took place behind secured doors in the old schoolhouse. The small statue was centered on a large plank table topped with a clean white sheet. The group was handpicked by Bishop Kenney himself, a select few. Each took his or her responsibility seriously. Jesse, Sara and Joshua, Ernie the cop, and Jay, back again for a few days, stood in silence in front of the chairs placed in a semicircle.

Everyone wanted to believe that the statue before them was the true Santo Niño. In respectful silence each one remembered how much the little saint had meant to them and their families. The *Niño* was like a brother who always understood and forgave, draping an arm around a shoulder or giving a strong embrace. They had grown up with the saint's image. Of course they would recognize him.

Doña Amarga sat in a worn recliner by the window, furious at being left out. She, after all, was the one who had opened the statue's box when it was returned. She had held in her hands the tiny treasure. How many times had she seen it in someone's home when a birthing was about to take place, or when someone was fighting their way out of a wasted body trying to pass on. So many had gazed on the Niño's loving face and felt strengthened for their leap to the next place. The midwife and healer suspected that Sara and Joshua were offended that she had opened the box without waiting for them. Fine. She did not need their approval to cure people or to bring new life into the world. Who did they think they were?

The expert consultants, C. Cruz Corrido and Dr. Sheldon Parkhurst, chosen by Bishop Kenney, wore white cotton gloves as they leaned over the table and prepared to examine the image. They inclined their heads toward each other. They looked like doctors preparing for surgery.

"How are you, Dr. Parkhurst? It's been a while since I have seen you."

"Fine, thanks. I see that your career as a 'contemporary' *santero* has taken off, *Señor* Corrido. Your carvings of the saints are in every gallery I visit."

"Thanks for the kind words, Sheldon, but remember that I follow the old traditions. I don't use ready-made paint or commercial varnish for my works. I make saints the old-fashioned way so that term 'contemporary' is somewhat misleading. It just means I am still alive." Corey looked deeply into Parkhurst's eyes and held his gaze for a long time as if asserting his status.

Parkhurst struggled to keep his expression innocent. He was not pleased when Corey used his first name. Parkhurst was rarely addressed by his first name, and not being called Professor or Doctor irked him. His expertise was seldom challenged. Nonetheless, Parkhurst kept a tight smile on his lips. When the best-known *santero* in the area chides you, Parkhurst told himself, keep silent.

Fr. Toledo, prim and austere in his long black cassock and white priestly collar, waited until the experts finished their greetings, and then asked the others to introduce themselves, mostly for his own benefit, so he could determine who was who. He led a prayer asking God and the Blessed Mother for discernment in their proceedings so that the members of the community could freely welcome their santo back into their lives. All eyes shifted to the experts. The melodious cooing of rock doves under the *vigas* on the porch produced a sense of calm.

Dr. Parkhurst stepped forward and separated the two pieces of the carving carefully, the figure and the chair. As he did before every lecture to his classes, the professor cleared his throat and raised his eyebrows, glancing around the room making sure that all eyes were on him. He began his analysis.

"The statue displays the usual characteristics of religious carvings made in the 1870s in New Mexico. The Santo Niño incorporates a number of symbols associated with the image: a seated figure of the Christ Child in the vesture of a medieval Spanish pilgrim, a ruffled collar worn by the prosperous young men of the times, a staff with water gourds attached, a basket filled with bread.

"Another important detail is the omission of a scallop shell pinned to the cloak which is important in statues from Spain and Mexico. The carvers often placed a scallop shell on the Child's cloak to indicate His status as a pilgrim on the famous pilgrimage road to Santiago de Compostela, Spain. *Bultos* made in New Mexico in the mid-to-late nineteenth century seldom have this feature.

"Furthermore, the carving is painted in the customary primary colors, red, yellow, blue. There is little modeling of the face. The orientation of the piece is frontal. The dimensionality is typical of the period.

"The carving, stylistically, reflects several aspects that had been noted by scholars in other carvings by Old Mister Benavídez. Although well-fed, this Child displays cheeks somewhat less rosy and rotund than normal. For example, the figure holds the staff with a few sprouts of wheat in his left hand. The hat has a thinner brim than most and the feathers are elongated. The eyes are bluish-grey, rather than brown. Eyebrows are outlined with black, and each of the bare toes is carefully carved.

"My conclusion, therefore, ladies and gentlemen," Parkhurst paused for effect, "is that this is the true image of the Santo Niño which disappeared from your chapel a few months ago." Smiles greeted the professor's words, and relief confirmed their best hopes.

When Corey stepped forward to examine the statue, his bearded face masked his expression. All present took a deep breath and listened attentively as he began.

"Dios les bediga. God bless you all. I want you to think for a few moments about everything you have ever heard about the Santo Niño which has resided for so long in this small *capilla."*

He waited for a long time before speaking again. "Do you remember anything your grandmothers or grandfathers or your parents told you about the image?"

"I know that it was responsible for many miracles. That's what my *mamá* always told us," said Ernie.

Jesse added, "My parents believed that its presence was a special blessing for the people of the village. When we did something bad, they used to make us ask ourselves what the Christ Child would have done."

Jay cleared his throat, his amber-green eyes filling with tears, "My mother said that if our family had prayed hard enough to the little santo, my father would not have died." Jay bent over to shield his face and turned his back to compose himself.

Sara and Joshua rose and held each other's hand. "We were told never to disrespect the image. When someone took it home for a special novena, their prayers were often answered."

"Does anyone remember anything else you were told about the image or Old Mister Benavídez?" Corey asked.

In silence, each one tried to remember what they had heard as children.

At length, Sara and Joshua stood up, holding hands. Their faces were as grey as their hair. "May God forgive us," whispered Sara. "We have forgotten something important."

Joshua continued, the painful realization tightening the skin around his eyes. "My grandfather told us," he paused, "that Old Mister Benavídez was so concerned about the statue he placed a curse on anyone who perturbed it."

Gasps and laments rose from the group. How could they have forgotten? Over time, when traditions are passed down orally, certain details are omitted. Who would have dared commit such a sin had they known of the curse?

The statue of the Santo Niño sat on the table, its chair supporting the figure of the Christ Child. Corey reached out with his white-gloved hands and picked it up gently. He separated the figure from the wooden peg that held it in place on the base and laid it on the table. Turning it gently, Corey examined the front, the back, and the bottom of the chair. Methodically, he moved a magnifying glass across the wood of the lower section. First, he examined the back side of the base. He glanced at the front section, the part that would be behind the seated saint's knees. Slowly he passed the glass over it. It revealed a few smears and showed a few nicks where the carver's knife had slipped.

Corey raised his head, peering over the dark-rimmed spectacles he seldom wore except for close work like this. For something so important, he put aside his vanity. So much depended on his evaluation. The room was quiet.

"Here is my analysis. The statue shows no damage. The pigments used are made in the traditional way and applied over gesso. There is little evidence of weathering. As Dr. Parkhurst observed, there is no scallop shell affixed to the Niño's cloak. The shell signified that the wearer was a pilgrim in medieval Spain on the route to Santiago de Compostela. My colleague's comment is correct that the shell's omission indicates that this is a New Mexican *bulto*, not Spanish or Mexican.

"I see few nicks on either section of the icon, the figure or the chair. The other symbolic elements are correctly used. The color of the santo's eyes is grey-blue, not brown. That is not consistent with other carvers of the 19th century. I find no evidence of the age of the carving.

"Most importantly, however, I find no evidence whatsoever of a hidden compartment in which the curse could have rested. Had there been such a compartment, one would see evidence of it.

"I, therefore, determine that this statue is not the original one carved by Old Mister Benavídez one hundred years ago and given to your chapel in perpetuity."

Corey replaced the figure onto the base and raised it high in his right hand.

"This statue is well-made and is, indeed, a Santo Niño. But, it is not *your* Santo Niño. This carving is a clever replica of the Santo Niño de Atocha."

Déjà Vu: Otra Vez

After Corey Corrido concluded his testimony, not a sound was heard. The others sat deflated and heavy. Each took the weight of the news as a physical blow that stole their breath. They felt their blood was draining from every pore. Shocked into immobility, they sat staring straight ahead.

It was an effort to get one's brain around what had happened. If the statue was a replica, then their own Santo Niño was still at large.

They had been taken in by a fake! Insult was surely added to injury. They had been hoodwinked. The search would have to begin anew. They were even more determined. It must be an inside job. The thief was one of them!

Father X rose and said, "Dr. Parkhurst, are you in accord with Corey's conclusion?" Parkhurst nodded his head and looked down. He was not used to being made the fool.

Corey came over to him and patted his arm. "You gave a good analysis, but you did not have all the evidence. How would you have knowledge of a lost oral tradition that was not forwarded on to this generation? How could you have known about the curse?"

The professor accepted Corey's attempt to take him off the hook but was too proud to tell him so. Without a word, he shook Corey's outstretched hand.

Fr. X seemed barely able to withhold a smirk. Just as he thought, these overly pious folk had been taken in by a fake. He shook his head, thinking of all the prayers that had been directed to an idol.

Would the *gente* never understand the difference between veneration and idolatry? Fr. X loved the Old Testament and gloried in all the stories of God's righteous indignation. The softer, more lenient, forgiving Christ was less to his liking. The God of Israel would have punished them.

"I will inform Bishop Kenney of the result of your deliberations," he declared.

The cleric gave a curt nod as he exited the schoolhouse. As he left, the realization that he was again in hot water with the bishop caused him to chew the inside of his cheek. He clenched his hands trying to hold down the burning liquid rising into his esophagus. He was determined not to expel it in front of the others.

The first to break the silence was Jesse. "What do we do now? Why would anyone go to all of the trouble of making a fake?"

"It is strange," agreed a subdued and pallid Joshua. "Now, more than ever, we have to find the original and discover the culprits."

Ernie stood up, his frustration finally allowed to erupt. "You all should have let the police know long ago. Now it's going to be much harder to track down the statue," he said. When he saw the baleful looks from Jesse and Joshua, he quickly added, "I do understand why the community wanted to solve the disappearance by itself. *Es una vergüenza para la gente.*"

Jay looked at his old friend and gave him a thumb's up for support.

Ernie shifted into his police persona, straightening his shoulders and drawing himself up as tall as possible. He put on an impervious, blank demeanor, just as in the old days so he and Jay could fake out the opposing football players.

"Jay and I will do everything we can to help you find the Niño and the *malvados* who did this. *Con su permiso*, I will talk to my superior, try to get a detective assigned to the case, and work to find the guilty party or parties."

Jay volunteered to type up a report on the results of the authentication meeting for the local archives and for the bishop.

"Now let's get down to business. Who actually found the bundle that was returned to the chapel?" Ernie looked at each person and noted his or her reactions.

Sara sat with downcast eyes as gentle tears fell onto the bodice of her simple cotton dress made from old flour sacks. "It was one of ladies, Mrs. Durán, I think," replied Sara, "but the one who decided to open the box was Doña Amarga."

"Who else was there? Can you tell me all the names?" Sara agreed to give Ernie a list of all of the ladies and children who had been at the church.

"We need to interview them, look at the crime scene again, and see if we can come up with any solid evidence. By the way, the fake, er, replica, will have to be taken in as evidence. It can no longer be displayed in the church," said Ernie.

"What about Filomeno?" he asked. "Any news?"

"I went the hospital to see the dear old man. Sadly, he is still in a coma." Jay cleared his throat as tears made a path over his high cheekbones. "You all know he was like a father, well – a grandfather to me." He paused, swallowed hard, and continued.

"His skin looks normal and the head wound is healing, but the doctors don't know how badly his brain was affected. Depending on the damage, Filomeno may not ever recall anything about the night he was injured. Keep him in your prayers."

"*Ay, pobrecito de él,*" Jesse added.

Jay went on. "Who's going to tell the community this latest twist? And, by the way, why wasn't Doña Amarga included in this gathering? She must be furious."

"Remember that it was the Bishop who chose the people for today. So, the *curandera* shouldn't be upset with us, just with the bishop," said Jesse. Everyone had respect – with a touch of fear mixed in – for the formidable woman and her powers. "Maybe we should just tell everyone by phone. It would be easier," offered Jesse.

"I disagree," said Jay. "Everyone in the village deserves the respect of hearing the truth from us all at once. Then people can ask questions."

"Telling the *gente* about this twisted trickery will be even harder than telling them about the disappearance. Now it looks like someone from Villa Vieja is behind this travesty," said Joshua. "And nobody likes to be *engañado.*"

"Apparently Father X is not going to take any action. He didn't even say goodbye. He just walked out on us," said Jay.

"I'll bet he's afraid of being in trouble with the bishop," said Jesse.

"*Vámonos,* let's tell everyone right away. We'll bring them back to the *capilla* tonight. Not a word about this from anybody.

Sara and I have to tell them the bad news," said Joshua. Ernie and Jay left the authentication meeting together in an altered state of confusion. Now what was going on in Villa Vieja? Nothing seemed the same.

Reverberations from Corey's assertion that the statue was a replica rumbled like a landslide as the leaders tried to make sense of this new twist. They left the darkened room and entered into the brilliant blue of a pristine December morning. Each was left to puzzle over the fact that their true Santo Niño was still missing.

Once again chapel bells called to Villa Vieja's residents. This time the news would bring further injury and insult. The nasty act of substituting a replica had made them look like fools. Only someone very angry at the Church, or with a huge grudge against the village, would do this. God was allowing them to suffer. It must be for someone's sins, but whose?

Tilting at Windmills

"What do we do first?" asked Jay as he and Ernie stood in the shadow of the *portal* of the old schoolhouse.

"I didn't have a chance to tell you before now, but I got word that I did real well on the exam. I'll be promoted to detective soon." Ernie smiled.

Jay gave his pal a big hug, "Way to go, Mr. Policeman!" I'm proud of you, bro. So, you may get to conduct your first investigation right in your old home turf."

"That has advantages and a few disadvantages, you know," Erne replied. "Everybody will try to find out from me what's going on, and I won't be able to reveal a lot. They'll see me as 'good ol' Ernie,' the kid from the canyon. But we have to find the statue and find out what happened here. It's important."

"What's your best guess right now?" Jay raised his eyebrows as he looked at Ernie.

"Not you, too? Hey, man, we need more real information. It's a big mistake to jump to conclusions. Besides, you gotta look at motive. It has to fit with the evidence."

"But, doesn't it look now like someone who is familiar with the church and the area did it?"

"Could be, but there's lots of if's. The trail is cold. We've got to go back and recreate the scene of the crime. Several things are going on here: the statue disappears, the Santo Niño is replaced, Filomeno is injured, and the replacement turns out to be a fake. It's not really our Santo Niño. It's a fake, a fac, fac–"

"-facsimile, a fake," said Jay. "Why? What's the point? And why did Filomeno get hurt? What does he know and will we ever know what he saw? He may not live." Just like old times.

Ernie made a quick Sign of the Cross. "But even if he does, he may not remember anything. We've only got few physical clues. We'll have to try to get fingerprints off the replica. That won't be easy."

"I heard the women cleaned up the chapel floor thoroughly. They didn't want even the slightest stain of blood left to remind them of what happened."

"That's why it's been real frustrating for me, this delay, with the novena and all," Ernie responded.

"Yeah, I agree, but you know, here in Villa Vieja, we've always needed the three P's – prayers, protection, and the police." Ernie shot Jay a disgusted look and continued.

"The public doesn't know how bad it is. You've heard about the gravestones and so on, and everybody blames the hippies. But the rise in property crimes of religious objects has been kept quiet. More than 24 churches and *moradas* have been vandalized."

"What? That's unbelievable! Are you kidding?" Thin frown lines creased Jay's handsome forehead. He let out a long whistle in amazement.

"No shit, man. The church doesn't want it known, but we learned in a briefing that since 1970, only two years, over 100 religious artifacts valued at more than $100,000 have been recovered from crooked art dealers and galleries. Not just here. Sometimes they ship the objects to New York or California. When that stuff gets sold to private collectors it's hard to trace. You can imagine that what hasn't been recovered is a lot more than that. This is big business, and it's not just our little *capilla* that's been hit."

"Are any of our infamous local *politicos* involved?"

"Not that I've heard, but you never know."

"Who has California ties around here? Well, I guess Dr. Parkhurst, some of the gallery owners, and Mando. Maybe that's why he disappeared a while ago. He probably still has contacts in California. He was a big Chicano activist, pretty well known around the L.A. area."

"I told you I heard Mando was back around here, didn't I?"

Jay nodded.

"OK," Ernie continued, "let's start from the beginning. It's a cold case now. I want to make a list of who to interview and figure out what physical evidence we can use, if any."

"I heard Sara was the first to open the chapel that morning, and she's the one who found Filomeno. She held his head. We could check her clothing for blood types," said Jay.

"We don't even know if Filomeno fell or if he was attacked," rejoined Ernie.

"Mrs. Mondragón is the one who cleaned the floor. That's good. She's so fastidious she saves everything. When my mother used to send me to her house, Mrs. Mondragón would make me wash my hands before I could sit down and drink the hot *atole* she always gave me. She, or someone, must have saved the blanket that was around the box."

"So, so far, we need to talk to Sara, Doña Amarga, Mrs. Mondragón, and the church ladies. Was Rosie Dawn there, too?" Ernie asked.

"No, Rosie told me she was at home cooking for the fiesta, but I think we should check out Harold and Paco and see what those young men have been up to."

"We should put Jesse on the list, too. He drove him to the hospital. Maybe Filomeno came to in the car or mumbled something about what happened," Ernie suggested.

"OK, we've gotta start somewhere. Let's make a list of all the physical evidence and who should be interviewed," agreed Jay.

Ernie and Jay were both methodical and took nothing for granted. When they finished, they had an outline of what to do:

a. Find out who had access to the keys for the chapel. (Sara, Joshua, Filomeno, Jesse?) Signs of forced entry. How many sets of keys? Where hung? New ones – check at Steinberg's Hardware.
b. Go to Frontera Hospital. Get in-take medical report, what injuries noted at admission. Find out F's blood type. Current condition. Possibility he might regain consciousness? Memory affected? Note: If he tripped and fell, no crime. Could be accidental.

c. Fiber analysis. Find out who has the blanket. Get expert to examine. Find evidence of what statue was carried in. (backpack? gunnysack?)

d. Perimeter check. Two months late. Very cold crime scene. Get photos of scene, area in front of chapel and behind, especially the door to the sacristy. Check windows, roof, doors. Get sketches. Collect any debris.

e. Prints. Shoe, boots in frozen mud, dust around altar, floor of chapel. Any residue of sole prints on chapel floor? Fingerprints.

f. Eliminate suspects. Always remember MOM – motive, opportunity, means.

g. List all persons in chapel on Dec. 11, the day of discovery of returned statue

h. Make list of persons of interest. Check out art dealers with record of receiving stolen property, gallery owners, collectors.

Ernie stretched and moved his head from side to side. "That's enough for now. Too bad you can't stay and help me with all of this." Ernie looked at his *compa'*.

"I'll be back when I can. I'll check out some of this from Tres Cruces," Jay promised.

Hermitic Encounter

As the search intensified for both the statue and the culprits, Jay felt impelled to hike to the top of Pilgrim's Peak before he left for Tres Cruces. He needed solitude and meditation, just as he had when he was a boy. Everyone was depending on him to help solve the mysterious disappearance of the statue. But he was confused, like the others, by the substitution of a replica. He had to sort things out. Jay was too perplexed by the events, especially the discovery of Filomeno's bleeding body, to think much about the hermit.

The beloved sacristan lay in a coma in Frontera. Would the old man have the strength to survive? The whole village was praying for him. But, who would remove the statue and replace it with a replica and why? Of course, the thieves wanted to sell the venerable statue, worth tens of thousands of dollars, but why put a fake image in its place? Figuring out the motive behind the theft should narrow the field of suspects.

After his three-hour hike on a steep, poorly kept trail that ascended 3,000 feet from the canyons below, Jay sat a while on the edge of the peak to enjoy the 360 degree panorama of the area. Pilgrim's Peak was the crown of the visible peaks in the area. Its distinctive outline of three elevations could be seen from all of the small villages nestled in the various canyons.

After a brief rest, Jay moved toward the place marked by three large crosses below which a spring bubbled forth. Ah, cold, refreshing water. He rested his angular body on a large flattish rock, stretched out his long legs, and took deep draughts of the water from his cupped hands. This water had special qualities – it not only refreshed, it healed.

Local knowledge said that when the legendary holy man, *El Ermitano*, as some called him, lived on the peak in the 1860s, there was no water on the mountain. People from the villages carried water to him. They also brought him the cornmeal he existed on. The hermit took pity on them and asked God for a favor. One day the hermit told two men to shoot a deer and, wherever it fell, they would find something special. Where the deer fell, the spring burst forth. Villagers believed that the water from the spring had miraculous healing powers.

It had been years since Jay had climbed the peak. He hoped he remembered how to find the narrow deer trail traced the edge of a cliff leading to the rock overhang that everyone called "the Hermit's cave." Deer were sure-footed, but was he? He was anxious when he saw how the roots of the piñon and juniper trees had smothered small boulders and made the trail even more treacherous. Jay focused his concentration on placing one boot before the other.

At last, he saw an overhang about eight feet high bending toward the southern slope. The shelter slanted to the back about 12 to 15 feet. Its back was the pink granite of the peak. Jay paused for a moment to catch his breath and to pray at the entrance. Stubs of burnt candles clung to the stone wall and lines of wax had dribbled down the rock like spaghetti strands. Jay's thoughts were of the hermit who had spent almost four years in this very place, a saint, some said, known as a healer. He had lived a simple life existing on water and cornmeal, a spiritual guide to those who sought him out.

Jay often felt those longings, too, to get away from others, to commune, to pray. Climbing the peak was exactly what he needed. As he looked toward the shadowed rock wall that formed the back of the cave, he noticed a piece of plastic caught under a rock. A Three Musketeers candy wrapper rested nearby. In a niche formed by the contour of the vertical columns, he saw a tin can that had been smashed flat, both ends cut out. Someone had been living in the cave, not just visiting. Of course, many people knew of the cave. Even after the hermit had left the mountain in 1869 to travel south into the Organ Mountains near Las Cruces, some families came at least once a year to pay their respects to his memory. Because of the spring, they could stay overnight and camp.

Jay looked around a bit more. In the far corner amid the rock rubble that covered the floor, he saw a glint of something metallic. He bent low under the granite overhang and moved closer.

He eased his long frame into the small space and knelt to peer at the object more closely, and then he reached for it.

"Nah. I wouldn't do that if I were you," a voice ordered. "Just put your hands behind your back."

Startled, Jay withdrew his hand. He recognized the voice that sounded as though each word had to be forced over pebbles to escape his mouth. Jay immediately recognized the man who threatened him.

"Don't worry, Mando. I'm just resting here. I'm going to turn around now."

He very slowly turned his angular body so that he could see Mando's form backlit at the cave's entrance.

Mando advanced toward him. When Jay saw his whole aspect, he was startled. Mando must have been fighting his darker demons. His long black hair lay in filthy curled clumps of ringlets. The skin of his swarthy face had a grey cast, and his brooding eyes were half hidden under drooping lids. Behind the feral menace in his eyes, Jay thought he saw a plea for help.

"What the hell are you doing here?"

"I guess I'd ask you the same question. Is this where you have been hiding out?"

"Nah. I'm not stupid. Too many people come up here. I know this peak better than anyone. But, there's more than one cave around here. You know that, too," Mando growled. He raised his haunted eyes to Jay's. What Mando beheld in Jay's strange green-gold eyes was gentle wariness.

"Is this where you hid the statue, Mando?"

"You think I'm the bad guy – just like everybody else. But, you're wrong, *ese*. I didn't hide it. And I didn't take it either, by the way. Besides, this is the first place anybody would look. How obvious can you get?"

"When I heard you were a big *honcho* in the *Chicano* movement out in California, I had to respect that. That took *huevos*, man. I figured you'd straightened out your life. My guess is that the anger and resentment you carried around like a load of firewood on your back got directed at the system, the man. Am I right?" Jay looked at him with calm.

"What do you know about being the outcast, bro? You were always the big star, the leader. Everybody loved you, especially the girls. But me and my buddies hated you. You made us feel like losers. You were, like, too good to be true. A little iffy. You know what I mean." Mando looked Jay boldly in the eye.

Jay blinked and lowered his eyes.

"So, what do you know about the disappearance of the statue and who took it?"

"I know plenty, but why should I tell you?"

"Maybe you could be the good guy for a change, help out the people in Villa Vieja."

"*¿Por qué?*" The question hung like a stalactite in the cave.

Mando advanced toward Jay, then motioned him to move out of the corner. Mando squeezed into the space to grab the glinting object. He picked up the solid silver raven with the turquoise eyes and rubbed it lovingly between his stubby fingers, nails packed with dirt.

"So, I found you," he said, looking at it. "Don't desert me again. I need you. The leather thong I hung you on must've worn out. I was afraid I'd lost you."

Jay was surprised to hear Mando express such devotion to anything. "What does that raven mean to you? Is that your totem?"

"What do you care? What if it is?"

"Everybody needs something to remind them of what they are – or what they want to be. I always keep a piece of wood that's shaped like an owl with me. My father found it in the forest and gave it to me not long before the accident. It reminds me of him."

Mando lowered himself down on the trail like an old man. Jay had smelled Mando's unwashed pungent odors inside the cave. Outside, the stench was bearable. Jay, tentative, sat down a short distance from Mando.

Both men sat on the edge of the trail, hanging their legs over the rocky ledge. Jay and Mando remained silent. The music of the wind rose from the canyons with a soothing sound as it played its songs through the needles of the evergreens.

The silence calmed their spirits.

Finally, Jay spoke.

"Mando, you helped out the *gente* before. Don't you want to do it again?"

"Why should I help those holier-than-thous? Those hypocrites don't see how un-Christian they really are. They jump to conclusions and are quick to blame. And they'll never change their opinion of me. They still think I'm the bad boy I used to be. You know they're stuck in their ways, with memories as long as a tether rope on a horse being broke."

Jay did not respond. Mando's oration gained steam.

"But, times are changing, *ese*. No more submission. It's time for us Chicanos to take our rightful place, a place of respect, just like the *guëros*."

Jay heard in Mando's rough voice his passion, his anger and, underneath, the pain of unhealed wounds.

"Look, Mando, we all have scars. Some have healed, some haven't. You found your voice in California. You inspired the *gente* to stand up for themselves." Jay paused and looked toward Mando. "And, you certainly impressed Rosie Dawn."

Mando glared at Jay, his face transforming into a feral mask.

"*Basta.* That's none of your damn business."

"Think about your raven, Mando. It was black and raucous, a force to be feared, a portent of harm. Now it shines silver in your hand. That's your totem, your spirit guide."

Mando continued to stare into the valley. He knew he smelled bad. He had been through tough times before. Now he had misplaced his desire to do good. He just did not care anymore. In his concentration, his aspect appeared as sinister and dark as before. The skin below his eyes was bruised purple. In the center of each pupil was a dark outline that looked like a fetus. Three parallel frown lines creased the space between his eyebrows. Mando's face tensed, like a predator's awaiting the exact moment to pounce. Let them go to hell.

"Here's what you might do to help find out whodunit. You could become the Chicano Colombo." Jay smile at his own joke. "From what I've heard, it looks like Harold and Paco have been up to something. How about going on a camping trip with them? Find out why they've gone 'camping' so often. They have been cagey about their whereabouts, and they know every cave in the canyons around here. Maybe they hid the statue for a while instead of trying to sell it. What do you say, *hombre*?"

Mando did not seem to be listening. He was wandering his own mental path. Another prolonged silence. Even the sharp bird calls from the irritable cobalt blue Stellar's jays high in the pine and spruce did not distract him. That sissy stuff Jay said about black to silver was good. Maybe it is my time to shine again. Finding out who's responsible for the statue's disappearance would be a start if I do want to redeem myself. I'm pushing 30 and don't have a life. Maybe César Chavez was right. He avoided violence and appealed to people's consciences and sense of justice. Look at the grape boycott! To even believe in that approach took balls.

Mando half-turned toward Jay who was still seated at a safe distance. "Maybe, when I make up my mind, I'll let you know. I ain't promisin' nothin.' "

"*Bueno.* I leave tomorrow. Talk to those guys. See what you find out," Jay added.

"I'm stayin' on the mountain for a while. How about you telling Harold and Paco I'm here?" His fierce look returned when he remembered he did not want Rosie to know how bad off he was. "Nah, don't tell them. Forget it.

"I might clean up in that miracle spring. Maybe I'll dress like the hermit in my big overcoat, carry a cane with a bell on it, and keep my hair long. They'll think I'm the reincarnation of the hermit." Mando allowed himself a slight smile, and Jay gave a relieved laugh.

"How do I get in touch with you? By the way, I may need a few bucks to get by for a while," Mando asked as he ventured a look at Jay.

"I've got a phone number. Here. You can call me collect in the evening." Jay fished in his pocket and found a twenty-dollar bill. He extended his hand toward Mando. "Take this."

Mando hesitated.

"You can trust me, Mando. I keep my word. But you know I'll have to ask Rosie what she's heard and whether she has any information. Are you two still, you know, together?"

"I told you, that's personal. Don't push it," growled Mando. "Listen, *ese,* I don't want Rosie to know we talked. *Ni una palabra.*"

"*Bueno.* I'll expect to hear from you when you've got something, not before. I'll try to be here for *La Nochebuena* in December. My mother's not doing too well. *Cuídate bien.*"

Jay stretched his back and got up. He knew better than to fence Mando in. Let him have his space in the hermit's cave. Jay knew plenty of other good places on the peak to think his own thoughts. His encounter with Mando gave him hope. Miracles might happen. He picked up his backpack and retraced his steps along the narrow trail. *Gracias a Dios.*

Mando stayed seated on the ledge and ignored Jay. He chuckled when he recalled how he had introduced Paco and Harold to a little weed when they were about fifteen. It might take a few tokes to get the information, but that would be fun. A Rocky Mountain high could be a kind of truth serum. Not a bad idea.

Mischief in the Mist

The lightness in his heart made Jay fly down the mountain trail. He descended the 3,000-foot drop in less than two hours.

What had happened between him and Mando? He felt pretty sure Mando would come through.

Muchas gracias, Señor. Jay realized he had just said his prayer aloud. Well, OK. Let the birds and rocks and trees and bears hear it. If Mando helped, they might be able to find out who had messed with the statue. Jay felt euphoric by the time he reached Rosie's.

As he neared, Jay heard sounds, like bells. Not church bells, he hoped. What could it be now? As he came down the path edged with stiff dried grasses, he saw strings of clear crystals hanging from the porch of Rosie's house. The cool breeze had set them into motion, and they chimed as they gently nudged each other.

"Anybody home?" he shouted.

"Just a minute, I've got dye all over my hands," responded Rosie. Her heart gave a few extra beats when she heard Jay's voice. "Come in and sit down."

Jay sat his tired body down on a couch covered with a brightly colored throw that he assumed Rosie had woven. He realized how sore his muscles were going to be from his hike up and down the mountain.

When Rosie entered the room, she was holding two cups of tea in her dark blue hands.

"Here, it's a mixture of herbs. You look like you might need it." Jay smiled his thank you.

"I went up Pilgrim's Peak today. I haven't climbed up there for a long time. Had to have some time to think."

"Did you figure out anything? It's so peaceful and soothing up there, not a soul around."

"Uh-huh," Jay muttered. "It was everything you said," forcing himself not to smile. He asked God to forgive his white lie. "Since I'm leaving tomorrow," Jay continued, "I wanted to touch base with you. Any ideas about who has the statue?"

Rosie lifted her head and her long hair draped each side of her face. She squinched her eyes and compressed her thin lips, making her look as severe as a disapproving schoolmarm. She seemed evasive and subdued.

"Well, I've heard that La Doña, or somebody, is spreading rumors that Sara and Joshua had something to do with it. She even accused them of hiding the statue so they could sell it later, when they get old. Since they are both single and have no children, they probably expect to be poor, although the community would probably take care of them, don't you think?"

"That's ridiculous!" Jay retorted. "The whole thing is a huge embarrassment for them. And Sara and Joshua would never do such a thing. They've devoted their lives to taking care of that chapel and everything in it."

"I agree, but La Doña's opinions influence a lot of people. People don't bother to think for themselves these days. If they hear something, they just believe it's true – and then pass it on to their neighbors. Lies rush down the mountain like a spring flood. Have you heard anything new?"

Jay took a deep breath, finished off his rosehip tea, and set the cup on a small wooden chest nearby.

"Rosie, I have to tell you this. Listen. Several people think Harold and Paco had something to do with the statue's disappearance. They're young, they have no jobs, and they have spent a lot of time away in the canyons, or so I hear." He sighed.

Rosie echoed his sigh.

"People wouldn't say anything to me if they were suspicious. He's my *hijito.*" Jay was touched to hear her use the fond term for son. Rosie contemplated the pattern in her skirt and said nothing.

"So?" The wood burning in the stove crackled. A shrill whistle of steam escaped from the teapot.

Rosie brought the teapot and placed it on the chest. She lifted worried eyes to Jay's. "You are my friend. I haven't shared this with anyone. I am beginning to wonder what Harold and Paco are up to. They don't tell me anything. I chalked it up to their age and their trying to become men. But I know Harold, and he's upset about something. He keeps to himself or goes over to Jesse's house all the time. I am so worried, but I didn't want to say it out loud. I haven't even mentioned this to Jesse. He would never believe that Paco, his adored son, could be in any trouble.

"And Paco," she continued. "Have you seen him lately? He's so thin. He used to kid around all the time, but now he's very withdrawn. Maybe even depressed. He looks like," Rosie paused, "a scarecrow, like his father. Maybe he's drinking or smoking something."

"I know this is painful for you, Rosie." Tiny creases appeared between Jay's eyebrows. "What do you think we should do?"

"We? Nothing." Rosie insisted. "Maybe when Ernie interviews them this week, something will slip. Then what? If Harold had something to do with it, they would run us out of Villa Vieja."

"Don't be so dramatic." Jay said, but he saw the fear in her eyes. It had been hard for her in Villa Vieja. "You should mention your concerns to Ernie. He'll know what to do."

"But what if the boys did do something?" The rims of her eyes reddened.

"As my father used to say, 'We'll jump off that bridge when we come to it.'"

A faint smile turned up the corners of Rosie's mouth.

"Let me know how it goes," Jay said. "You have my number in Tres Cruces. I'll try to be back for *La Nochebuena*."

Rosie's eyes brightened briefly, and then flickered out like a candle in a breeze. "Good. I'm glad. Maybe by then our little saint will have wandered back. Who knows?"

"We should start getting some answers now that everyone knows. It's probably someone from around here. The sooner we find out, the better. People are on edge. I can feel it."

Jay rose to leave. Rosie met him halfway. They hugged in a strong embrace, more than friends, less than lovers.

"Goodbye, *Rosa querida.* We'll find out why the statue is gone. By the way, is Harold here? I'd like to say goodbye to him."

"He's out, as usual. I'll tell him you asked about him."

Jay and Rosie stood for a moment near the door and gave each other another *abrazo* before Jay ducked his handsome head under the low doorframe and stepped out into the moist velvet darkness. As he walked to his mother's house, he glanced up at the dark outline of Pilgrim's Peak and smiled.

After Rosie shut the old blue painted door, she fixed herself another cup of tea. When she needed to think, she sat in her own comfortable chair, the one she offered to guests. Jay's warmth remained in the cushions. Hearing Jay's suspicions that Harold might be implicated disturbed her. She replayed Harold's behavior over the last few months.

Harold had celebrated his eighteenth birthday in June. He was officially an adult and legally responsible for his actions. If he did take the statue, it was almost certain that Paco was involved. Neither of them would do something like this alone. But, the two of them had gone on plenty of long backpacking treks in the wilderness areas. They had been gone almost three weeks once. She flashed back to their conversation when Harold had returned from that adventure. Rosie had been sitting on her porch weaving a new design she had created when she heard him.

"Harold, you're back. I was so worried about you!" Rosie dashed down the steps to greet him. When she heard herself, she was chagrined at the triteness of her greeting. She was not usually so conventional, but she had said what mothers were supposed to say. Harold gave her a perfunctory hug.

With her arms wrapped around his waist, she was surprised at how much taller Harold was. He must be at least 6' 3" by now, she thought. He looked like an outdoorsman, a real mountain man. His ragged beard, a dark reddish brown, felt soft when she patted it.

It was hard to wrap her mind around the fact that this was her little boy.

"Well, come sit down, and I'll fix some fried potatoes and venison that Jesse brought over. So, where did you go? Tell me about it. How was it? Did you see any big animals up there?"

She noticed how rough the skin on his hands looked and saw several small cuts on his right hand as she led him to the kitchen table.

"Do you have any coffee, or some milk? I'm really thirsty."

Rosie hurried to put the coffee pot on the stove. "It'll be ready soon. The water's already pretty hot."

"Thanks, Mom." She felt a glow of pleasure when he called her that. She was not one to allow her offspring to call her by her first name, a practice many of her hippie friends had.

Harold took a long sip of coffee that she had fixed just the way he liked it, with fresh cream.

"We saw lots of deer, a few bald eagles, and an elk. We took a bow and got a deer the second day so we field-dressed it and then hung it up to dry. Boy, it got tough. The next night a bear must have smelled the meat."

Rosie's almond-shaped eyes opened wide with concern.

"The bear came into camp. He was so close to the tent, we had to throw him some meat to deflect him. We got some pot lids and banged them together to get him to leave. He got our whole stash. So, that was pretty exciting." They both laughed, Rosie out of relief.

"Paco and I decided we'd better stick to smaller game, rabbits and squirrels, something we could eat up quickly. There were lots of wild gooseberries and raspberries, too. Man, they were so sweet, well – not the gooseberries. We'd taken canned meat and beans, onions and potatoes, and a few peaches, so we ate OK."

"What did you guys do all day? Didn't you get bored?" Rosie asked.

"You know how everything takes more time when you're camping, making the fire, cooking, setting up. We just hung out or we explored the upper parts of Cougar Canyon. Paco always brings his harmonica. At night, we sang loud enough to scare off any big animals. We did some whittling." Harold stopped. Rosie thought she saw his skin redden a bit.

Harold changed the subject. "So, Mom, what did you do? Did you miss me?" He gave her a silly, crooked smile.

"Of course. I always do. Well, I designed a new pattern for a wall hanging I want to weave. I caught rides to town with different people. I bought some seeds. The weather was good for the garden. We had some rain. After the air is washed clean, you know how it clears up. With all the clouds, we had magnificent sunsets. Did you and Paco get wet up in the canyon?"

"Yeah, we got soaked a couple of times, but we just took off our clothes and put them on bushes and waited for the sun to dry them out. Oh, one day, we had a big surprise. We heard something coming. We kind of held our breath – it was Jesse. He found us somehow and stayed a couple of days. He's a really neat guy. I like him, and he is a good father to Paco. Jesse gives us advice and tells about the old days and how he was raised."

Rosie noticed the flush of wistfulness that washed across Harold's fair skin. She attempted to suppress the guilt she felt about the lack of male role models in Harold's life. His own father had never once tried to make contact with them. Of course, they had moved to the western edge of the continent. Still, Harold was his son.

"OK, so when's dinner? I have to go over to Paco's."

"About two hours or so. Be back before dark. I'll make your favorite, *posole,* tomorrow, with blue corn and *chicos*. It takes a long time to cook."

"See you later, alligator." He flashed a peace sign as he went out. How silly that boy-man was.

As Rosie cut up onions and garlic at the heavy kitchen table, she was surprised that Jesse had not mentioned his visit to "the guys." She rolled up the sleeves of her dark green sweater and rinsed the *cilantro* in the sink. Once again, she tried to remove the dye from her hands. Her fingernails were still outlined in blue.

God help me if Harold had anything to do with the vanished statue. Dear sweet little saint, please don't let my son be involved, but, if he is, then I beg You to forgive him, she prayed.

She wondered if she should tell Ernie. Harold and Paco had been away the day the replica was discovered in the chapel. Rosie had stayed home to avoid Doña Amarga. Instead she made a big batch of *posole* for the fiesta of Our Lady of Guadalupe the next day. Sara had told her the *curandera* had opened the bag right there in the chapel. Everyone knew that Sara and Joshua were not happy about it. Rosie knew firsthand that La Doña was not afraid to use her power when she needed to.

The light blue water in the basin colored the metal a hue that reminded her of California and the ocean. She went to the small side door and swirled the water to throw it on her winter garden.

She missed Jay already.

Iconic Investigations

Ernie arrived at the Frontera Police Department which was housed in an ornate 19th century red sandstone building with carved arches over the windows and not enough electrical outlets. He checked the FBI's Uniform Crime Reporting (UCR) listings for recent reports of property crimes of religious objects in the vicinity. There were several, but none mentioned a Santo Niño. He chatted with a couple of his officer pals in the understaffed station. They had heard nothing.

The Frontera station was always shorthanded. Ernie's sergeant had ordered him to follow up on the Villa Vieja investigation on his own time. They had too few cops as it was. His superior pointed out that, as of yet, there was no concrete evidence of a crime being committed or a police report. Ernie would have to use his skills, unofficial and unpaid.

Just in case, Ernie contacted one of his pals in the *barrio,* one of the West Side gang, a sometimes snitch named Horacio. On a partially paved street surrounded by run-down adobe houses, Ernie caught up with him.

"Hey, Horacio, have you heard anything about an old statue from the canyon being stolen lately?"

"No, man. My guys are into TVs, radios, stereos, jewelry, bikes, watches, stuff we can sell. We wouldn't touch those old saints sitting around on our grandmothers' mantels. Don't you know about honor among thieves?" he grinned. "No way. Besides, our grandmothers would twist our ears and never forgive us. We don't know nothin' about art stuff."

Ernie was convinced it was unlikely that his *vato locos* had anything to do with the statue. "If you hear anything, let me know."

"You got it, Mr. Policeman."

Ernie decided to proceed and treat the matter as if it were a crime. He sat at his and Jay's old picnic table in a nearby park and began a list of things to do – on his own time. A lot of work for no pay, but he understood.

Ernie's instincts made him a good cop. After dealing with plenty of liars and scam artists, he was good at detecting lies. He knew when he heard a cover-up or a half-truth and was expert at reading body language. If Jay were still around, we could play good-cop, bad-cop and get to the truth right quick, he thought. It was great to have Jay back in the extended family of Villa Vieja. He and Jay still cared about the same things.

Time to check on MOM – means, opportunity, motive.

Ernie pulled out the list of motives he could think of for the saint's disappearance. He had jotted them down on a crumpled sheet of lined tablet paper.

1. Greed, money. Most likely. For drugs? Desperation?
2. Revenge. Someone who hates priests.
3. Anger at the church. Feels slighted. Priest or bishop involved? Ridicule the beliefs of the faithful and their devotion. Embarrass church leaders.
4. Jealousy. *Envidia.* Smear or embarrass the *mayordomos*, church leaders. Someone who feels ignored. (Jesse, D. Amarga?)
5. Pure cussedness. Cause pain and trouble.
6. Loss. A woman or girl mourning a lost child (stillbirth, abortion, natural). Someone "borrowed" statue to replace a lost baby. Ask Doña Amarga for help with this.
7. Acquisitiveness or status. Museum, collector, desire to acquire something sacred, beautiful, historical. Follow up on leads.

Ernie had his unpaid work cut out for him. Better get started. Back at the station, he finished some paperwork and helped himself to several sugar-coated donuts someone had dropped off.

Start with the power structure. It was simple – talk to the big community leader, Doña Amarga, then others on his list. Since he'd grown up in Villa Vieja, he had a healthy fear of La Doña himself. He decided to begin with the most difficult interview, Doña

Amargarita. She was the one who always knew who had stolen the apples from her tree, knocked over the outhouse, and which mischievous boys had tried to peek through her windows at night to see the *espantos* in her back room. It was said that she had powerful allies in the spirit world, and that's why she could heal others. No matter how, as a boy, when Ernie had denied his *pecaditos* she always knew. He was still somewhat intimidated by her, but he was a big boy now. He'd arranged to see her that evening. Let her call on all her allies to help Villa Vieja find the culprits.

The twilight sky was a soft mixture of gold and blue haze when Ernie set out for her house. From high perches on the cottonwoods near the river a pair of owls hooted alerts to each other. Doña Amarga's old tin-roofed adobe house was hidden by thick willows near the river. He remembered how all the kids thought it was spooky.

As Ernie stepped on the worn planks of her *portal*, a shiver passed through his bulky body. Get a grip. You're a grown man. The owls had triggered memories of the fear he felt when he and Jay would sneak through the woods, dared by their friends, to see if they could see the ghosts who visited her. He pounded his fist on the solid old door.

"Doña Amargarita, it's me, Ernie Lucero," he called. He waited. The floorboards creaked in protest as she clumped toward her front door.

"*Pásale.*" The woman was formidable. The old door creaked as she pulled it open. Her bulk filled the entire doorframe.

"*Gracias. Buenas noches*, Doña Amargarita. How are you?"

She did not answer and waved him to a chair at the kitchen table. The kitchen smelled of smoke, the tang of roasted chiles, and something sweet, like cedar or incense. Circles of soft light formed halos around the candles set around the room. They cut the gloom.

"How are things with you, *Señora?*" He greeted her again.

"About the same as always. You want some coffee, tea? I got hot water."

"*No, gracias*. Don't trouble yourself." Although in Villa Vieja niceties usually preceded business, Ernie decided to get right to the point. The *curandera* sat impassive, massive as a tree stump. Ernie reached inside his jacket for his notebook.

"*Bueno*, about the Niño's disappearance... I need your help. We have got to get to the bottom of this *vergüenza*, for everybody's sake."

She nodded.

"May I ask you some questions? You are the person who unwrapped the bundle in the chapel on the day the replica was discovered, *verdad*?"

"Yes, and it's about time someone came to talk to me, especially after nobody invited me to the meeting when they found out it was a fake." She folded her arms over her massive breasts. The look in her eyes challenged him.

"I believe you should have been invited, Señora. Perhaps the bishop just forgot. His Excellency has many things on his mind."

"Ha!" she snorted. "He's just afraid I have powers he doesn't have. *Pues*, what do you want to know?"

"Describe what you saw in the chapel on December 11 when the ladies went to clean for the feast of Our Lady of Guadalupe."

"When I got there, Sara was sitting on the floor holding Filomeno's bloody head in her lap. She told me, 'Go get Jesse to bring his big car to take him to the hospital. And call Joshua.' I started out as Gracia was coming up the path, so I told her to call Jesse. I went home to get my bag of *remedios*. I did what I could for the *pobrecito*. He was not conscious, and he was very cold."

"What did you notice in the chapel? Was anything missing? Did anything seem out of place? Was the stove turned on?"

Ernie felt he was rambling.

"Wait, let's do this." Ernie started over. "Tell me first everything you remember about Filomeno. What were his wounds? Could you tell where the blood had come from? Was his body near the gas stove? I was told there was blood on the floor. Where else did you notice blood?"

"That's a lot of questions," said Doña Amarga. "I saw that Sara's skirt was stained because she was holding his bloody head. I wiped his face with a cloth dipped in herbal waters. I still have the rag I used."

Ernie looked at her with approval. "Keep it. We may need to examine it later."

She continued. "I didn't see no blood on the stove. There was some on the kneeler of the back pew, you know, the one that belongs to the Mondragón family?" Ernie nodded and made a note to check on this.

"How do you think Filomeno was injured, from what you saw?"

"He wasn't near the stove. He was more to the center. I guess he stood up when he heard something. Maybe he tripped on the kneeler, or somebody pushed him. *¿Quién sabe?*"

"How did you know he was alive?"

The *curandera* shot him a dark look and snapped, "Do you know how many years I been taking care of the sick, the injured, and the dying in Villa Vieja? Thirty-eight! Of course I could tell he was alive!

"When Jesse got to the chapel, Joshua was in the car with him," she continued. "They picked up the old man and carried him to that big old Cadillac. I guess Sara decided she didn't want be left out, so she went, too."

"Was Filomeno on his back or stomach when you ministered to him?" Ernie asked.

"He was on his back. Sara must have turned him over. He's very frail. Good thing his neck wasn't broken. She could have killed him. She moved him."

Ernie could not help but notice the scorn in Doña Amarga's voice. He'd heard there was ill feeling between the *mayordomos* and the *curandera*.

"Any bruises or cuts?"

"He had a big knot on his right temple, big as an egg from a goose. Lots of bruising around the eyes. His lips were blue."

"Any other injuries on his hands or legs?"

"Not that I saw. He was unconscious, that's for sure."

"*Bueno*, now tell me about the canvas bag. Where was it when you first saw it?"

"Down beside the altar where it's always kept unless somebody has borrowed it. Mrs. Durán discovered it. She yelled for me to come see. The bag was like a soldier's, about the size of a small pillow. It had something hard inside. It could fit into a gunnysack or a backpack, I guess."

"Tell me about what was inside."

"A wooden box wrapped in a blanket."

"Who has it now?"

"Mrs. Mondragón has it. She keeps every scrap of cloth and paper she gets her hands on. You should see her *casita*! It's stuffed full, like a big *burrito*."

Ernie interrupted. "Did the blanket look familiar?"

"It might have been an old army blanket. It was wrapped around a wooden box with a latch. The Santa Niño was inside on a deerskin lining. Nothing was broken that I could see."

"How did Sara and Joshua react when they came back and found out you had opened the bag holding the statue?"

La Doña puffed up like an irritated horny toad. "*¿La verdad?* They were very upset with me, and still are. I don't think I did anything wrong. We didn't know what it was, so we opened it."

Ernie understood her defensiveness. "You understand the reasons people do things. People tell you many secrets, *qué no?* Doña Amargarita, do you have any idea who took the statue or why?"

"I have my own ideas, but the answer has not been revealed to me yet. I am keeping my mouth closed for now." She gave Ernie a coy glance.

Ernie stifled a smile. Everyone knew she was a *mitotera* whose tongue wiggled and tattled. She probably did know. He jotted a note to keep her on the list of suspects.

"Thank you for your time, Doña Amargarita. You have been very helpful. If you recall anything else, *por favor*, let me know right away. We will find out the truth."

Moving Targets

A few days after his conversation with Jay, Mando prepared to leave the mountain. He washed his filthy hair, tied it back with a piece of leather thong, rubbed his silver raven with fingers still showing ingrained dirt and located the old trail down the northwest side of the mountain that led to Cougar Canyon.

I'll track Paco and Harold until I find them. Mando knew where he'd stashed food in several rock ledges in that area. Tucked into the inside pocket of his heavy overcoat was enough *marijuana* to encourage a truth-telling session with the boys. I'll find out what they know and where they hid the statue and make them take me there. He envisioned the relief and joy that would greet their arrival in Villa Vieja when the people heard the news. The local bad boy would be vindicated. He was beginning to enjoy the vision.

Maybe it was time to step up and try again with Rosie. However, the underside of this plan was not so good. Rosie Dawn would blame him for fingering Harold, her dear son. He would decide how to deal with that complication later.

Before he descended from the mountain, Mando got down on his knees and prayed the only prayer he could remember. "*Senor, ten piedad de nosotros.*" Mercy had not been a part of his vocabulary for a long time, but he knew he needed it now. He was ready to say goodbye to the revenge that weighed down his heart.

He raised himself, shook his head, and glimpsed a large fallen branch that would make a good walking stick. He knocked off some bark and made a smooth grip. With the red-handled Swiss Army knife that Rosie had given him, he shaved off the little knots and protrusions. Mando shouldered his stained backpack, grasped the walking stick, and moved toward the faint path that led down the mountain. Just then, the sun made a brief appearance above the clouds, etching the day in gold.

That night, Doña Amarga sensed disturbances in the air that woke her repeatedly throughout the night. Indistinct and mysterious as the mists that rise at twilight along the curve of the river, dark images grew into menacing shapes above her. She raised her arms to ward them off. At her window, a huge glossy blue-black raven pecked at the glass and flew out of sight. It returned with a silver nugget in his beak. It dipped, peered with a severe eye at her and headed away toward the tall tips of the evergreens that fringed the distant skyline above Cougar Canyon. Doña Amargarita was unsure of what this visitation portended.

Jay said goodbye to Rosie in Villa Vieja and left for town. He felt duty-bound to check on Filomeno before he departed. He parked his fully-loaded truck, Hi-Ho, near the hospital and found his way to Filomeno's room.

When Jay drew the curtain back from the bed, he gazed at the discolored face of the dear sacristan. He felt warmth on his prominent cheekbones, unwanted tears tracing pathways to his mouth. They tasted salty. When Jay looked into the old man's eyes, he saw glimmerings of images becoming clearer with each moment, like particles caught in amber.

Jay held his breath.

"Ja-, Ja-, Jacinto, *mi'hito*, is it you?"

"I am here," spoke Jay with emotion.

"*Estoy contento*," said Filomeno before he lapsed back into another world. Jay wiped away the tears and sought out Filomeno's doctor.

The doctor affirmed that there had been a few signs that Filomeno might come out of his coma.

"Remember, though, we have no way to know if the patient will have memories of that night in the chapel. He may never regain either his long-term or his short-term memory. We will have to wait and see."

Jay adjusted his leather hat as he walked back toward Hi-Ho patiently waiting in the parking lot. He gave a long, fond look toward the mountains that cradled Villa Vieja and all its secrets. He had plenty to mull over as he set out for the long, lonely drive to Tres Cruces. Oops, he'd almost forgotten. He had one last errand. He swung by The Span and bought six donuts – three cake, three glazed – and a bag with a dozen *empanadas* filled with spiced tongue and *piñones* for his trek. If there were any left, he would share them with his special friends.

When Jesse heard the news that Filomeno had regained consciousness briefly and had mumbled a few words to Jay, he knew the time had come to act. He hurried to remove the work tools from his truck and replaced them with his camping gear. He had to get in touch with Harold and Paco as soon as possible. He tied his favorite horse, Junior, to his truck and drove the rutted road to the trailhead of Cougar Canyon. There he left his truck hidden behind a grove of willows, untied Junior, and rode into the canyon.

Not long after, he found an empty campsite. He felt the heat escaping from the embers in a ring of stones. He recognized some of Harold and Paco's gear and a pair of his own muddy work boots half-hidden under a neighboring piñon tree. He figured he would just wait for their return. The enormity of the danger filled him. The young men's futures depended on the news he brought.

Jesse crossed himself. He closed his eyes and prayed so intently that his whole body arched in supplication.

Finally, he grabbed his tent stakes and pitched a small canvas tent on a grassy area near a bushy juniper. Magpies with their bold black-and-white patches flew about searching for food. The rat-tat-tat of a woodpecker looking for tasty morsels in the bark was the last sound Jesse heard before he drifted into sleep.

When Harold and Paco returned, Jesse woke and tried to convince them that they had to come forward. The boys were easy targets of suspicion. Some whispered that they were *malvados,* betrayers of the village. He told his beloved son, Paco, and Harold, who was almost like a second son, that they were becoming outcasts. The young men refused to believe how badly the village wanted retribution for the disrespect that had occurred. Jesse told them that hiding out only fueled people's suspicions.

Although Jesse also told them about Filomeno's condition, they refused to realize they were in jeopardy if Filomeno's memory returned. The young men ignored his urgings. Angry that he could not persuade them, Jesse yanked out the tent stakes, rolled up the tent, and loaded it onto his saddle. As he rode back to the truck, his anger and fear did not subside. He hitched Junior to the truck and drove home in the coldest hours just before dawn.

Back home, Jesse flopped onto his bed fully clothed and slept fitfully. Nightmares came back as usual to torment him. One image was of a strange creature, half-man, half-beast, running. He couldn't dispel the image of Mando that flashed through his mind. Where was he?

Higher up in Cougar Canyon, Harold tried to cheer up Paco.

"Listen, bro, you gotta eat. You're getting thin as a beanpole. Here, I brought some granola with cranberries and nuts, the kind you like."

Paco looked at Harold with sad, listless eyes and pushed away the bag of snacks. "I can't think of anything except what's going to happen if Filomeno dies."

"They don't know who did anything," Harold said. "You've got to stop worrying. You look really bad. That alone will make people suspicious. Take this. Eat it on the way back to camp. *Vámonos.*"

Weeding Out the Truth

Mando easily found Paco and Harold's campsite in Cougar Canyon the next afternoon. Surprised, they invited him to stay for supper. Mando set up a flimsy tent.

In the twilight's blush after supper, Mando, Paco and Harold sat on a high rock ledge, legs dangling in the vivid air. Far below them, blue spruce and white fir formed patterns of light and dark. Paco and Harold looked dazed and dreamy as they shared puffs on the dirty-brown, hand-rolled cigarettes. Under Mando's tutelage, they had learned the art of getting pleasantly high. Occasional bitter flakes of weed stuck to their lips and tongues. The acrid taste reminded them that what they had done would have repercussions. Mando urged them to take another toke.

Harold and Paco both remembered the first time Mando had brought the two of them to this secluded section of Cougar Canyon on a camping trip. They had been, what, fifteen? Both had felt anxious about being so far from the village and doing something bad. Neither would admit his fear and covered it by assuming the swagger of not-quite-men. With Mando, they were not on their own in the wilderness. Mando introduced them to this guilty pleasure, his gravelly voice intoning directions.

"Inhale slow and deep. Hold the smoke in your lungs as long as you can. Exhale slowly through your mouth. Try to breathe the smoke back in through your nose."

Harold thought that Mando had said "longs" and wondered at first what he meant. He smiled at this memory now and glanced over at Paco who seemed finally to relax.

Mando broke the silence. "*Bueno*, it's time to talk about something serious with you two." The rough, bumpy quality of

Mando's voice seemed different today. It sounded more like a deep purring growl. Mando took a long time before his next words came.

"I know you guys know that these hippies around here come and take anything they see lying around – an old wagon wheel, a crooked saw, and a rusty bed in an abandoned house. They take anything, man. They're even stealing from the f-ing churches! They steal the little fences from around the graves, grave offerings, even the tombstones from the *camposantos*. That's sick! Those are relics of our ancestors, our grandfathers and grandmothers. Do you have any idea how much they can sell the stuff for, especially the religious statues?"

Mando peered through the haze at them. Both boys avoided his piercing stare. "I hear that if you know the right people, you can sell this stuff for thousands, maybe tens of thousands of dollars. Why should those guys – or anybody else," he paused, "profit from this stuff, bros? It's our *herencia*, yours, mine. It's a disgrace to the *raza. ¡Punto!*" Mando snapped his fingers so loudly that Paco and Harold both flinched.

"OK, *ahora, dígame*! Exactly what do you know about the statue's disappearance?"

No one spoke. Strips of rose and ocher clouds turned dark grey and midnight blue. In the silence that followed, the first owls began their calling as the wind played faint tunes on the green needles.

After a long time, Paco spoke. "That's crazy. Do you think we'd do that, man? Why? The *gente* would be furious. They might even attack whoever did it. That Santo Niño belongs to the chapel. My papa told me the story about how it came here."

Mando leaned forward and held their eyes with a hard look. "Don't give me that shit. You know exactly what I'm talking about. People are saying you two took the little statue of the Santo Niño from the church. Where did you hide it? And what did you think – that you were going to sell it? *Qué vergüenza.*"

Paco and Harold looked at each other and widened their bleary eyes. They tried to come out of the fog and back to reality, to an awareness of how deep the drop-off from the ledge below would be. The natural forest smells were masked by the pungent smell of marijuana. As they tried to focus on Mando's face, it seemed sinister and darker than before. He looked at each of them with the eyes of a panther. In the dark circles that were his eyes, they saw the outline of a fetus in silhouette. Mando's face tensed like a predator's, waiting for the exact moment to spring.

"How could we have done it? Who'd carve the statue?" Harold asked, noticing how hard it was to fold his lips to shape his words.

"You're a great carver, Harold, and somebody else could have helped with the decoration. In the village, some of the men learned the way the old *santeros* made carvings. All that stuff they used is from around here. So, *dígame la verdad*. Who stole the statue and where is it?" shouted Mando.

"Why do you care? Everybody says you hate Villa Vieja and the people there!" shouted Harold.

Mando recoiled, "Who said that, your mom? Does she believe that? I have been fighting for my people for years. They just don't see it." Sadness softened his dark flesh.

"Now, where did you hide the statue? Nobody knows these canyons like I do. I've spent half my life in up here alone, hanging out, following trails, shooting deer and wild turkeys. I saw a herd of mountain goats once. I've even seen a bull elk mount his lady friend. I know every cave and hiding place around here. Why did you do it? Did you get tired of being *pobrecitos?*"

They both nodded without thinking. They knew how it felt to never have enough, to be always thinking about money, never buying anything fun. Their single parents struggled to make a decent living.

"I want to know who did this. Now."

"Taking the statue wasn't our idea. We would never sell it. The one who did it is going to be black-balled forever, maybe even ex-communicated."

Quick as a jackrabbit, the world had tilted. Their footing was uncertain. Paco shot Harold a look to shut him up, afraid he was going to rat someone out. He had to stop him. He took a swing at Harold's startled face. As Harold ducked, Paco swayed woozily. They tried to balance themselves.

"What the...?" Harold didn't know what to do. He'd never seen Paco like this. Paco's face was set in an all-encompassing grimace as the gears turned the situation over and over in his head. Harold knew that look. Paco processed things slowly. He wouldn't say a word until he was ready. He could be pricklier than a burr in a boot.

Mando was passionate about Chicano rights. Harold had heard his powerful speeches, but he had never seen him so worked up. Mando, the "bad boy," was accusing them of being criminals. Could they trust Mando with what they knew? He seemed mellower, not as tough. Maybe it was the marijuana.

Mando said, "Why don't you two chill out and talk things over? I'm going to take a leak. I'll be back."

He left them and went to his lair next to the juniper tree. The young men's words and behavior had convinced him they were deeply involved in the theft and the assault. He hunched his shoulders and leaned into the shadows. If he could help them decide to tell the truth and confess, he'd get some respect. He figured they needed time to talk.

Mando was surprised at how much Paco had aged. He looked beaten down, like a dog cowering before his master's kick. He was thinner even than his dad. Another scarecrow in the Fuentes family. Harold seemed jumpy and quick to anger. Mando was convinced they were hiding something big.

Whose Clues Accuse?
January, 1973 – Villa Vieja

Ernie's suspicions about Harold and Paco needed to be based on more than their frequent absences from the village. There could be many reasons why they stayed away. Ernie knew there must be some clue that would either link the young men to the crime or exonerate them. Ernie had already done a perimeter search around the chapel. It yielded nothing. Since unseasonably warm temperatures had melted most of the snow, he would look for new evidence.

One Saturday morning in late January, Ernie rose early and assured his wife he would be back in time to take their boys to a movie called "Charlotte's Web."

Dressed in Levis and a heavy flannel shirt, leather jacket, and his favorite old hat, a dark-stained Stetson with a thin ribbon band, he left the house. Since the investigation was not yet an official police matter, he was not obliged to wear his uniform. Good thing. The pants were getting a bit too tight around the waist.

Before leaving Frontera, Ernie stopped by The Span, ordered a large coffee and three cinnamon cake donuts to go. He set off for Villa Vieja. The interior curves of the road, still in the shadow of the mountain, were icy, so he took them with care.

When he rounded the last curve just before the village, he saw Pilgrim's Peak in all its magnificence. He wondered if it held secrets about the Santo Niño. No use going up there in winter. The trail was too dangerous. Frigid winds blew at 10,300 ft. A climb would have to wait until spring. He prayed that the case would be solved by then.

Ernie parked his truck on the dirt road south of the village chapel and started walking downstream. After a half mile or so, he had seen nothing but a lot of mud. He turned around and started back upstream. Villa Vieja was quiet as he passed the village. Twists of smoke rose from rusted tin chimneys into the crystalline air. He imagined the families sitting around their wood stoves, trying to stay warm.

When Ernie passed the chapel, he asked the Santo Niño for help, and headed toward the path along the river that carved into dark shales and grey limestone deposits bit by bit, carrying away tiny particles in its flow. Nothing lasts and everything changes. That was hard to get used to. Nostalgia for "*los tiempos pasados*" affected the old and annoyed the young. His people had survived here for hundreds of years. Nothing to worry about.

The sun was strong and soon Ernie was sweating. He took off his Stetson and ran his chubby fingers through his hair. He wanted to stay out of the mud so he chose to walk beside the path on wet masses of matted grass.

After a few minutes, Ernie sat down on a dead log to enjoy a rest and his first donut. Patches of snow lay in the shade of the trees. As he got up, his eye caught the glint of something metallic in a patch of snow to his right. When he bent down, he saw that it was the buckle of a wadded and semi-frozen canvas backpack. He already had his gloves on, so he lifted the sodden mess and put it into the burlap bag he'd brought along in case he found something. This might be what the intruders had carried the statue in. When he looked at the ground where the backpack lay, he saw the outline of a boot print frozen in the mud. He pulled his measuring tape from his pocket and noted the dimensions. With a small camera he had remembered to bring, he shot that print from several angles. His buddy in the police lab might be able to determine the make and size. He looked around the area carefully, put his Stetson back on and treated himself to the last two donuts. He patted his *panza* and smiled like a Buddha. It was worth giving up his Saturday morning, after all. The day was a success.

Back in Frontera, he called his buddy at the police station and got the favors he needed. Once the results were in, Ernie would confront Jesse to see if he recognized the backpack or the print of the boot. Ernie believed that now they would find the culprits. Then he would advise Jay. His *compa'* would be proud of him.

Spilled Beans

Jesse had wrestled with the angel of guilt for almost three months. He knew what had happened the night of the return of the replica. If only there was some way to change the folly of that evening!

How could such a well-intentioned act have such dire consequences? He bore the burden with stoicism, a characteristic of those who live hard lives. He begged the crucified Christ to forgive him. As yet, there was no evidence that his prayers had been heard. There was no one to whom he could unburden himself. How he missed his wife at times like these. Even in her twenties, Carmela had been wise and calm. That Paco had grown up without his tender mother to shape him pained Jesse. She would have understood.

Jesse was caught between the thorns of the cactus and the daggers of the yucca. Since Filomeno's assault, he had worn a hair-shirt for penance underneath his work shirt. He knew who was really responsible for the removal of the statue. The consequences were serious. The results of his actions so weighed upon him that Jesse felt like an ox pushing a millstone.

The time had come for the *verdad*. Since Filomeno had opened his eyes and spoken a few words to Jay, the truth might soon escape. No more delays. The old man might regain his faculties, after all. For those who had prayed every day for his recovery, it was blessed news. For Jesse, it was a threatening possibility. When others around him had prayed for Filomeno's recovery, Jesse merely mouthed the words.

Jesse was glad it was Sunday. He had slept until mid-morning when the sun finally awakened him. He started a fire in the wood stove. The cabin warmed up. After some clean-up chores, Jesse put the cleaned beans into his old iron pot and cooked them for a few hours, feeding the stove more wood as needed. Like the coffee pot, it had had plenty of use.

Jesse remembered that Rosie had given him a jar of *salsa de chile* she had made "from scratch," whatever that meant. He dumped in a big ladle of the fiery mixture. That should warm up the body. Jesse had already sliced some potatoes for *papas fritas*. The hot lard was smoking. When he dumped in the potatoes, the grease crackled and spat, so he put a flat tin lid on top of the frying pan. He heated himself another cup of coffee in the chipped blue enamel pot smudged from the many times he had used it over a campfire to make cowboy coffee.

It was mid-afternoon when his dogs, Tico and Taco, began to bark. Jesse heard some commotion in the front area. What was it this time? Last fall, a cougar had eaten one of his neighbor's calves. He'd better go see. He kicked off his fur-lined slippers and put on his heavy work boots. By the time he got to the door, he heard voices. When he recognized them, a big smile illuminated his thin, ruddy cheeks. A flush of pleasure warmed him. Paco and Harold were back. After they'd fed and watered the horses, they would come in. It was lucky Jesse had dinner almost ready, and there was plenty to eat. Maybe he'd even make biscuits if there weren't enough tortillas.

When the figures of three men filled the doorway, he recognized his son and Harold, but who was the long-haired, grimy one? The three turned in concert and looked toward the stove and the welcoming aromas coming from it even before they greeted Jesse. They looked famished. Jesse hugged Paco and Harold and gave each of them a few solid thumps on the back for good measure. His "boys" were here. The third man held back for a moment and then extended a hairy hand.

Jesse was baffled by the appearance of Mando at his door in the company of Paco and Harold. What did his presence mean? Jesse knew that Christ had told His followers to honor strangers and treat them with respect, so he would try. Jesse was, after all, the *hermano mayor*. It was his Christian duty. But, ask him in?

"Mando, I was just thinking of you today. *¿Cómo está?*" Jesse shook Mando's hand which swallowed his thin one. "*Bienvenido.*"

"Thanks. I'll bet you're surprised to see me, *¿qué nó?*"

Jesse avoided the question and motioned him in.

After the men finished supper, they sat around the kitchen table and had a beer or two.

"So, *dígame, por favor*, how did you all meet up? Where were you, Mando?" asked Jesse. "No one has heard from you in a long time."

Harold jumped in. "Mando's a good tracker. He came looking for bad guys and he found us. He tried to get us to confess," answered Harold. Jesse wondered what he was talking about. Since when was Mando doing anything for Villa Vieja?

"He had a peak experience with a jay," added Paco. They all three cracked up.

Mando pushed back his long hair. "Well, let's say the hermit made me do it."

Jesse was still puzzled. This was not the Mando he'd heard about. Jesse began to get a bit *enojado*. Everyone was in on something but him. He didn't like being left out.

"What did you tell him?" Jesse muttered. The line between good guys and bad guys seemed to have blurred.

"Mando decided to help find Villa Vieja's missing statue and came after us. He thinks we stole it for the money. We told him he was wrong," explained Paco.

Before Jesse could make sense of what had happened, more serious barking outside signaled another visitor. Now what?

A knock on the door ended their conversation. "I'll get it, *papá*," said Paco.

When Paco recognized Ernie, his pallor increased. "*Buenas noches.* Come in."

Harold jerked his head toward Mando. "Did you rat on us?" he demanded in a stage whisper. Mando, as surprised as the others, shook his bushy head.

"*Buenas noches.* What luck to find you all in one place! That makes things easier." Ernie entered with Jay right behind him, looking tired and subdued. "Jay's here as a witness. I asked him to come."

Harry and Paco made room for the visitors in wary silence and angled their bodies away from the cop. Something big was about to happen.

"Siéntase." Jesse offered Ernie a beer. Jay shook his head.

"No, gracias. My *panza* is too big already," Ernie chuckled. *"Está tarde. Perdóname,"* he apologized. "I took my boys to the movie in Frontera and then came back to Villa Vieja.

"Bueno," he continued. "We are here on business. I have found new evidence, so I called Jay to come back. We need to talk to you about what happened on December 11, the day on which Filomeno was found bleeding in the chapel, the same day a replica was placed behind the altar by someone, or ones. Although no charges have been filed, we have been directed by the *comité* and my superior to carry on the investigation of these matters. That is what we have done."

Ernie opened the duffle bag he had brought and fished out a wrinkled, dirty backpack wrapped in plastic. He held up the misshapen object.

"Does anyone recognize this?"

Silence.

"It has the initials 'FF' stitched inside the flap," Ernie prompted.

In the distance, they heard a coyote howl.

"How about this?" Ernie held up the diagram of the boot print. Anyone here wear Tread-On-Me work boots? Paco, could you hold up your feet so I can see the bottom of the boots you're wearing?"

Paco looked like he was going to faint. In a choking voice, he spoke out.

"That's my backpack, and I was wearing my *papá's* boots that night."

Jesse gave a warning look at his son, lines of worry creasing his face.

"Don't listen to him. He's trying to protect me." Jesse gave a loving look at Paco and announced, "It's time for everyone to hear the *verdad*. Things are not the way they appear."

Jesse offered Ernie a cup of coffee which he accepted and drank black. He knew would be a long time until he got back to Frontera.

Anxious to defend his friends, Harold started. "You blame us and nobody even knows for real why the statue disappeared. OK, so, around a year or more ago, Jesse took Paco and me camping. He wanted to discuss an idea he had with us. He said he'd need our help."

Paco interrupted, "My *papá* just wanted to do a good thing."

Harold nodded. "Jesse said he'd heard that the Church could close down rural chapels like ours. He was worried, but the older men told him, '*No te preocupes*, it'll be OK.' But the possibility kept bugging him, right, Jesse?"

One look at Jesse's flushed and contorted face confirmed it.

"He told us first," Harold continued, "that he wanted us, but mostly me, to make a copy of the Santo Niño, just in case something like that happened. He knew I loved carving and he knew some stuff about how the *santeros* made their statues. He knew a couple of carvers he could ask about details. I wasn't too sure I could even do it. But I like challenges and I wanted to help, so I agreed."

"Are you sure Jesse didn't just put you guys up to this so he could sell the original and make some money or that he wanted to substitute your copy to fool the people?"

Enraged, Paco jumped up and advanced toward Ernie.

"You take that back, you *pendejo!* My dad would never do something like that. He gives all his time to the village and the church, and nobody even notices or thanks him."

Harold grabbed his friend around the chest and pushed him back down onto his chair.

But Paco was angry. "My father was not even born here but he loves the Santo Niño, and he knows the story of how it was given to the *gente*," he shouted. His breathing slowed to faint gasping sounds like a baby sucking an almost empty bottle.

"Paco didn't mean that. He's just really upset about this whole mess," apologized Harold for his friend.

Ernie was used to outbursts and dismissed it with a flick of his hand. He addressed his next question to both of the boys.

"So, what was your understanding of what would happen to the fake statue?"

"Jesse said that Plan A was just to hide the original and keep it safe for the people of Villa Vieja in case the Church took everything from the chapel. He knew it belonged to the *gente* and not to the greedy priests or even the bishop," said Harold.

"It was early October when I went into the chapel just before dark and took the true statue, Jesse admitted. "I wrapped a blanket around it and put it under my overcoat. I'm skinny, so there was plenty of room for both of us. I kept it in my house in a very safe place. But when the people missed the *Niñito* so much, I got the idea of putting a replica in the chapel for them."

Paco added, "That was Plan B."

"Where did you go to make the replica?"

Harold and Paco spoke in unison. "There's lots of caves and we know them all." They looked at each other with surprise. "Jinx, you owe me a Coke," chortled Paco first, socking Harold on his upper arm.

Harold added, "We never moved the original from Jesse's. We just sketched its shape. Then I'd carve it when we went camping and come back and do the details here."

"So, assuming you are telling the truth, what happened to the original by Old Mister Benavídez?" Ernie was dogged in his pursuit.

Jesse stood and began pacing. "The old ones say always begin a story at the beginning, so here goes. Last year at the meeting of the *cofradía, los hermanos* heard that what had been rumored was actually happening. The bishop had closed down some chapels not too far from here. I was afraid we might be next."

"Again, I repeat: What happened to the original Santo Niño then? What did you do with it?" pursued Ernie.

"I got so worried I couldn't sleep at night!" Jesse crossed his arms and rocked back and forth. "Ask Paco. He knows. He heard me. I had nightmares. I would even cry. I figured it could happen here, especially since Fr. X didn't like our ways or devotions."

"Why didn't you tell the *majordomos*?"

Jesse lowered his head. Embarrassed, he mumbled in reply. "They're old and I didn't want to upset them. They might not believe me or trust me anymore. They don't really know much about what's going on outside of the village."

"Is that the whole story?" Jay asked.

"Well, since they are the direct descendants of the carver, they might think they owned it and should keep it themselves."

Jesse knew in his heart he was jealous of them, too. He broke into the raucous sobs of a man not used to crying.

Mando, Jay and Ernie averted their faces. The story that was leaking out made them rethink some of their assumptions.

"I had almost finished the replica," Harold went on. "Paco and I had to spend a lot of time up in Cougar Canyon so we could decorate it. We thought nobody would know. We spent so much time his girlfriend got mad and broke up with him."

No one laughed.

"Jesse decided it was time for Plan B, so Paco and I put the replica back in place of the real Santo Niño. Jesse had removed the real one and hidden it. Nobody would know the difference. The people could still pray to their little saint. After all, they were praying to the Baby Jesus, not the statue."

Jesse shifted his angular shoulders and twisted them to loosen the tightness.

"It was getting close to the end of the novena in December," he said as he took up the story. "I thought that would be a good time to substitute the copy so the people could be happy again. I got the key and gave it to them," he pointed his chin at Paco and Harold. "They would leave the replica in the Niño's special place later that night. Then they were supposed to lock the door and give me back the key. I kept the original Santo Niño here *en mi casa.* I knew it was a safe place to keep it from harm.

"I waited and waited for them to come back that night. When they didn't, I knew something had gone wrong." Jesse leaned back in his chair and closed his bloodshot eyes. "*¡Ay, Dios mío, que lástima!* So I took the original to the *morada* and hid it."

"Everything seemed OK," Harold continued. "We got into the chapel. The door was unlocked. We figured somebody forgot to lock it. We went through the back door into the sacristy. I was on the altar platform ready to put the bag with the replica in its space under the altar when we heard something.

"Paco stepped off the altar platform and moved closer to the pews to see what made the noise. He was nervous and so was I. We heard a shuffling noise.

"Who's there?"

"We both got scared. I almost wet myself. I shoved the bag into the space and whispered to Paco, '*Vámonos*,' but he just stood there, like he was frozen."

"Filomeno saw me," wailed Paco. "He knew it was me. He just stood there looking so sad and disappointed. I was upset. I didn't think. I just wanted to get rid of that look. I moved toward the voice and shoved. There was a thud. I didn't mean to hurt anybody!"

Harold took up the story again. "We high-tailed it out of there through the back door and ran toward the river. We ran as far as we could. When we stopped for breath, Paco threw the backpack down, and then we ran some more. We were afraid to go to either of our homes that night. We just huddled up in the hay in an old barn and slept until daylight."

No one in the room spoke. They were busy trying to sort out the ironies of how what seemed to be a well-intentioned act had gone wrong. Usually God brought good out of evil, but their actions had backfired and brought injury and strife. Moreover, and Filomeno could lose his life.

Ernie the cop, impassive, broke the silence.

"Let me remind you all of the possible criminal charges that might result from the acts that were committed that night. Even if all you have said is true, there were unlawful acts with bad results. First of all, however, there was no unlawful entry into the chapel since Jesse was allowed access by his position."

"Legally, all the persons involved, Jesse, Paco, and Harold, can be charged with the same crime and be found equally culpable. Although Jesse was not present for the taking of property and the assault on Filomeno, he was the mastermind of the plan. If this matter goes to trial," Ernie paused to see the effect of his words on the trio, "the sentence will depend on the evidence and proofs submitted. The court also has to consider what it calls 'mitigating circumstances.'"

Ernie shifted his weight. His hips hurt from sitting so long, but he resumed his role as interrogator. "Paco, in terms of intent to harm, according to your own words, you pushed Filomeno.

"Was it your intention to disable him from pursuit? If so, it was criminal intent to harm. You told us you just reacted. Did you intend for Filomeno to have a concussion? The issue is whether the injuries were intentional or accidental. Given the severity of the injuries, the charge could become aggravated assault – which is a felony."

Paco seemed to shrink into himself, as he sat, hunched forward, head in his hands, diminished and moaning. The room had grown colder, and Harold put a couple of logs into the stove and sat down. He patted Paco on the back.

Mando had already heard most of what Paco and Harold had told Ernie when he was smoking pot with them. He had urged them to come clean. Mando now understood why Harold and Paco's behavior had changed so dramatically. They were scared witless with guilt and fear. He remembered that feeling from his "bad boy" days.

Well, no triumphal entry to the village with the miscreants in tow. No entry like a *conquistador* marching the natives in chains to meet their punishment. Too bad. He'd have liked to be the hero. But Mando had gotten them to tell the truth and face it. He knew Rosie Dawn would be crushed when she heard about Harold's involvement. Mando had his own apologies to make, but he knew he was not quite ready.

Ernie continued his explanation of the legal aspects.

"If Filomeno regains consciousness and remembers his assailant, he could bring charges. If he wakes up and has lost his short-term memory, obviously, he can neither condemn nor forgive. If, God forbid, Filomeno dies, the situation is more complicated. The charge could be manslaughter in the first degree which bears a penalty even if accidental. If the intention was to injure, the charge could be criminal assault or pre-meditated murder." Ernie paused and drank the last of his cold coffee.

"The other witness is Harold. He saw Paco push him," commented Jay.

Harold looked alarmed. He hadn't thought of that. He stared at the fire through a tiny window of glass. Flames erupted suddenly and then died down. The embers glowed like red-eyed monsters.

It was time to put their stories together. Ernie spoke slowly.

"*Bueno.* Jay drove seven hours to meet me in Frontera – just the two of us – so I could ask you about what I found. I came back to Villa Vieja tonight to clarify what happened on the night of December 11th, and to find the *malvados* who took the statue. After hearing each of your versions of the events that night, I still have several questions.

"First, Paco, does the backpack with the letters FF belong you? Your baptismal name is Francisco Fuentes, *qué no*? Is the backpack I found near the river what you carried the replica in that night?"

"It is," Paco admitted with reluctance. "My godmother sewed the initials."

"OK. Second, Harold, whose work boots was Paco wearing that night, his or his father's?"

"Paco said his were getting too tight, so he borrowed his dad's boots from the closet. I saw him."

"So, it was Paco, not Jesse, in the chapel that night?"

"Right."

"Jesse, I need you to verify that the work boot print diagram I showed you shows the same Tread-On-Me brand as yours."

"It does," confirmed Jesse.

"Now here's the biggest question, Jesse. Who knows where the real statue of the Santo Niño is right now? Is it intact? Can you show it to us?" He glanced at Jay. "We'll see if what you've said is true."

Jesse knew it was time for confession. "It's not here. It's in a safe place. It's too late tonight, but I can take you to the *morada* near the old creek bed where it's hidden. Then you'll believe me."

"You mean it's right here in the village? OK, Jesse. I'll pick you up here about ten o'clock the day after tomorrow, Tuesday. You will show me the statue. I will bring Sara and Joshua as witnesses. We'll call a meeting of the village so you three can tell your stories to them.

"Since no police report has been filed, the *gente* of Villa Vieja will decide what to do after that." Ernie stood up and the others were relieved that enough had been said.

The embers were cooling, and grey ash lessened their glow.

Much had been disclosed. How much of it was true? Each man faced his own dark night of soul-searching.

"*Me voy,*" announced Mando. He rose with feline grace, stretched, and excused himself. He shook hands all around and went out into the moist night air that comforted him. He knew where he could stay. He knocked at Doña Amarga's door. When she opened it, her hair stood around her head like an electrified white halo. The silver raven glowed against Mando's bronze skin.

Doña Amarga was not surprised that Mando had finally returned. She had seen a raven in a vision, and she knew about transformations. She opened her arms and embraced him. Her *Mandito* was back. She got out the *colchas* and a pillow and handed them to him.

"Water's still hot. You can wash up. *Hasta mañana.* I'm going back to bed." When Doña Amargarita lay her heavy body down on her big feather mattress, she thanked all of her familiar spirit helpers who had brought him back, especially the Santo Niño.

Mando needed more time to decide when to visit Rosie.

As Ernie left Jesse's house to return through the dark mountains to Frontera, lenticular clouds stretched across the face of the moon barring most of its light. Things were not always what they seemed. He should know that as an officer of the law.

The stories he and Jay had heard from Jesse, Harold, and Paco held together pretty well, but he still had reservations. Motive was everything, and it had to be clear. Was the incident that had caused so much pain and embarrassment really done for righteous reasons? If there were no theft, if everything the trio said was true, was there was any crime at all? Did the real statue rest nearby after all? He would know on Tuesday when Jesse took him to the hiding place. What was undeniable was that Filomeno was injured. The question of how badly remained.

Ernie's head was throbbing from the evening's surprises, but he was too tired to think about what he and Jay had heard to discuss it any longer. He said a grateful goodbye to Jay who'd left his truck at Ernie's house. Jay didn't even come in. He gave Ernie a thumb's up as he steered Hi-Ho out the driveway for the long drive back to Tres Cruces. Jay knew that Ernie had been right to insist that he return to witness the trio's reactions to Ernie's accusations. While they could still deny everything, their confessions tonight would not be based on Ernie's word alone.

When Ernie went inside, he kissed his sleeping sons and traced a small cross with his thumb on each of their foreheads, hoping he would never be in a situation like Jesse's with either of them.

With Contrite Hearts

Harold decided to stay over at Paco's house. He called Rosie and said he'd see her the next day. His best friend was in trouble. So was he. He had gone along with the idea and made the replica. What now? Would people believe their confessions about why the statue had disappeared? Maybe it was time for another prayer to the Santo Niño to set things right.

Exhausted from the emotional drama of their encounter with Ernie, the trio knew that hard choices had to be made. They couldn't keep their secrets any longer. Harold knew he and Paco had to support each other and Jesse. All three were bound together by the same rope. Any one of them could loosen or tighten the pressure for the others.

Up in Cougar Canyon, when Harold and Paco heard that even Mando believed they were guilty and he was going to "take them in," their world turned upside down. They had become the bad guys. Harold realized how serious things were and urged Paco to 'fess up. Paco's guilt was literally eating him alive. Harold was afraid he might starve himself to death. He urged Paco to face what his anger had made him do and pledged to stick by him. So they had come down from Cougar Canyon, Mando striding beside them, his long black hair bouncing with every step.

Paco was seated on the lumpy sofa staring at the paint peeling off the front door. He saw Harold shifting from one foot to the other waiting for someone to say something. Paco had been in conflict long enough. He had to face what his actions had done.

Paco stood up and crossed to Jesse who was in the kitchen area putting away what remained of their meal. The tears he had tried to quell insisted on running down his face.

"*Papá*, I am sorry to bring this shame upon you. I didn't mean to injure Filomeno. I didn't think. I just reacted. This whole mess is because of me. *Perdóname*. Can you forgive me even if Filomeno doesn't?" Paco's skin was ashen. His sobs erupted as he slumped to the floor.

Jesse leaned down to embrace his son.

"*Cláro que sí, mi'hito*. I am the one who decided to replace the Niño with a copy. If I had just hidden the original in a safe place, none of this would have happened. *Fue orgullo mío*. I was afraid to share my ideas with anyone. I thought maybe they would laugh or tell me I was *loco*. My pride made me want to receive all the credit for saving the Santo Niño. *Fíjate,* if I had just trusted the others or not been so selfish none of this would have happened."

Harold joined in the hug.

When they sat down, Harold's voice trembled when he asked, "Don't you think the people will believe us? What we did wasn't bad. We tried to safeguard Old Mister Benavídez's piece from harm, or worse, destruction."

"*Pues... No sé*. You know how people are," Jesse replied. "They like to think the worst sometimes. Who knows? Even after I show Ernie where I hid it, they still could think we did it for the money. For me, the worst is what could happen with my son's future. Why did God let this happen? That is the most difficult."

Both young men were surprised to hear Jesse's laments. Neither thought anything could shake Jesse's faith in God.

Harold, trying to lighten the heavy air, announced, "Tomorrow I have to face my mom. She'll be happy that I wanted to do something good and proud that I carved the replica, but she'll be furious that I didn't tell her anything. In fact, I had to lie a few times about what we were doing or where we were going so she wouldn't get suspicious."

Jesse composed himself to reassure Harold and everybody else. "When I can, I'll talk to Rosie before everyone finds out what happened. I'll explain that it was my idea. By the way, how did Mando get involved with you two again? There were rumors that he was around. He seems mellower. Was he really going to round you up and bring you in like the white-hatted sheriff in a western?"

Paco glanced at Harold, "Shall we tell Papi everything?" Paco smiled.

"Sure, we might as well."

"Mando came into camp to find us, but, get this. Mando ran into Jay in the hermit's cave. Jay convinced Mando to help in the search – by convincing him it would be a good way to redeem himself with the village – and to find out the real story from us. Jay knew we were up to something. For some reason, Mando decided to do it. He suggested that a little "truth serum" – that's what he used to call the *mota* we smoked with him – could get us to tell all we knew. So, he trailed us. He's like a panther. He found our camp."

Jesse harrumphed and thought that, no matter what, Jay always came out looking like the hero.

"Mando found us," continued Paco. "We all got high and, I guess, we told him the truth. But, Papa, we didn't tell him about you. We told him it was our idea. He didn't hear the whole story until tonight with Ernie."

Jesse looked at the two young men, a rueful half-smile on his long ace.

"Gracias, mi'hito," he said.

Jesse stretched his long legs and cracked his knuckles.

"Basta. Enough 'palaver,' as they say in the westerns," he said as he yawned. "We each need to do one very important thing Tuesday. We have to visit Filomeno. *Dígale lo que necesita oír.* Tell him what you have to, whether he is conscious or not. Ask him to forgive you. It's going to be hard." Jesse let Tico and Taco in for the night. The faithful dogs consoled them all.

"Is his head all bandaged? Does he have black eyes or bruises still?" Harold didn't want to see his injuries.

"I don't know. It's been almost a month now. I've seen him only once since the incident, the accident. That's all I know," Jesse replied. *"Qué más?* Oh, yeah, ask God to forgive us, too."

The winter sky was clear on Tuesday morning, and the sun felt strong when Ernie arrived about ten o'clock to pick up Jesse, as planned. Harold and Paco would go in the old Cadillac straight to the hospital to visit Filomeno.

After Tico and Taco barked, they recognized Ernie's scent and quieted. When Ernie stepped onto the porch, all he heard were loud snores. He would have to wake them all up. He yelled, "Hey, here come the police!" He had to laugh at his own joke.

Harold and Paco roused themselves and took Jesse's truck to go the hospital. Jesse went with Ernie to show him the saint. They agreed to meet up later at the hospital.

Hospitals are holy places where the living honor the still living. A quiet respect prevails, and the ever-present smell of cleanser emphasizes the purity. Paco and Harold entered Frontera Hospital with trepidation. When they asked, the friendly, middle-aged nurse with three brightly-colored clip-on butterflies in her ash-blond hair informed them that Filomeno was still in Room 2. She guided them down the white hallway. A thin curtain partitioned his space from the next bed.

Harold and Paco pulled up chairs. Filomeno looked like a small child. His deep sunken eyes were closed, and his breathing was regular but faint. A clear IV tube was implanted in his arm.

"May we touch him, just take his hand?" asked Harold.

"Sure, if you're gentle and wash your hands first. He is still in a coma but there are some signs that he may regain consciousness. Ring for me if he wakes up, opens his eyes, or seems to have any trouble breathing." The nurse left the two young men alone.

Paco and Harold had agreed that when one of them was ready to speak, the other would leave the room. Privacy had long been a necessary component for confession. When Harold indicated by pointing to the door with pursed lips that he should leave, Paco smiled. Just like the old men in Villa Vieja, his friend Harold was getting pretty Hispanicized. Paco went outside.

Harold scooted the chair closer to the bed and took Filomeno's cold, bluish hand. It felt like a dead trout. He took a deep breath before he began.

"*Señor* Filomeno, please don't die." His voice wavered. "We all want you to come back to us. I don't know if you remember how you got hurt. I want you to know that my friend, Paco, didn't mean for you to get hurt so bad. I don't know if you can hear me. I know God is watching over you, especially the Santo Niño. We're sorry for what happened. Please forgive us. That's Paco, his father, Jesse, and me, Harold, Rosie Dawn's son. That's all. Amen."

Harold thought he felt a tiny quiver, but it was hard to tell if it was his hand or Filomeno's. Harold felt wobbly as he got up to call Paco in.

Paco's skin had new lines. His heartbeats were irregular, and his hands were sweaty as he placed his skinny body in the chair. He sat for a few moments next to Filomeno's bed. He was so weak he felt he might faint, but he had to confess.

"Señor Filomeno, it's me, Paco, Jesse's son. I know you can't hear me, but I have to tell you that you're here in the hospital because of something I did. I can't explain it all, but I pushed you and you fell down and hit your head on a kneeler. It shook your brain. I am so sorry. I was scared. I was just trying to help my father save the Santo Niño. It got all messed up.

"Could you please try to forgive me? I will take care of you and help you for the rest of your life if you just wake up. Could you also please ask God to forgive me? He knows you love Him more than I do."

Paco paused and took a deep breath. "If you hear me, squeeze my hand."

When Paco leaned closer, he thought he felt a quiver. He put his ear close to Filomeno's lips. The old man was trying to say something. It sounded like *"egote asolbo,"* and then, *"Ya me voy."* Paco understood only the second part.

Paco was still shaking when Harold came in.

Putting his hand on Paco's shoulder, he said, "Let's go get some air."

Grateful for his friendship, Paco went outside with him. They sat on a bench and felt the force of the winter sun burn away some of their guilt as they waited for Jesse and Ernie to arrive.

Ernie was deep in his own musings. He followed Jesse as they clambered over cobbles in the old river bed that led to the abandoned *morada.* Strange events had taken place in Villa Vieja. Ernie's profession trained him to be suspicious and skeptical of collusion among suspects. He was in his cop mode today. Deep down, he wanted to believe that the purloined statue and Filomeno's injuries were the outcomes of good intentions, that of safeguarding the Santo Niño. Still, the statue in the *morada* could be the replica, after all. Ernie patted his gun. He didn't think Jesse was trying to dupe him – or was he? This had better not be a wild turkey chase he thought, compressing his jaw.

Ernie had intended to ask Sara and Joshua to come along as witnesses then realized that the rocky, uneven footing would be dangerous for the elderly brother and sister. When he heard that Corey was in town for a demonstration of techniques used by the old carvers, Ernie decided to use him as a witness instead. Corey would recognize his saintly little friend right away.

A turkey vulture glided overhead, scavenging. Dead grass and a few leaves crunched under their boots. Winter crows settled in a black cloud on the pines nearby and cawed for attention.

The two men picked their way around cobbles and big branches. They followed the path people walked to pray the Stations of the Cross. Rounding the bend, three large crosses loomed in front of a long rectangular adobe building that had only one door and a few narrow windows hidden under the eaves.

Jesse led the way to the door. Ernie stood, arms folded, as Jesse stepped forward and put a long key into the rusty lock. The lock did not open on the first or even the third try. Ernie was dubious that it would open and wondered if he'd been set up. His patience was waning, but, at last, with a squeak, the heavy door swung inward. They made the Sign of the Cross before they entered.

Dust rose from the packed earth floor. It was wintertime, so there were few furnishings or ritual objects. What looked like a simple altarpiece held only empty *nichos* and a few booklets containing old *alabados* sung during Holy Week.

"Remind me about this building and what it's used for," said Ernie.

"The Penitente brotherhood uses it mostly just before, during, and a little after Holy Week. Otherwise, the *cofradía,* of which I am the *hermano mayor,* uses it. We provide food and clothing for those who need it and we store the supplies here. We also use it as a place for meetings and for special prayers. It works out."

Jesse disappeared around the wooden backdrop behind what resembled an altar.

"Come here," he called to Ernie.

Ernie moved to Jesse's side and watched as he removed a knife from the tool bag he had brought. With great care, Jesse ran the blade along a small seam in the wall. He cut twice vertically and twice horizontally, making a rectangle about 3 x 4 feet in size. Jesse pulled it forward and removed it from the wall. Boards formed a space inside the wall. Jesse reached in and lifted out a khaki bag. He zipped it open. Inside was what felt like a box. It was wrapped in an army blanket.

In silence, Ernie watched as Jesse removed the wrapping and laid it on the floor. Inside was a wooden box with a metal latch tied with a leather thong.

"Shall I open it?" Jesse asked.

"Not if I'm taking it to Corey to verify that it's the original. You know, Corey never explained what the missing evidence was that convinced him that the returned statue was a fake."

Jesse said proudly, "I can show you. Then you will know for sure that this statue is the real one, and I have told you the truth."

"OK, let's see it," replied Ernie.

Sure enough, resting on a piece of deerskin inside the box was a statue of a seated figure dressed as a medieval Spanish pilgrim with a large plumed hat, holding in one hand a staff with dangling water gourds and, in the other, a basket with loaves of bread. His bare toes peeked out from under his gown.

Jesse picked up the *Niño* and gave it to Ernie. "Hold him tight. I need two hands to do this," he said.

Ernie reached for the statue. He held the image of the Child Jesus with both hands as though it were a newborn. A sense of peace seemed to travel through his hands into his arms. It radiated throughout his whole body as he held the Santo Niño de Atocha.

Overwhelmed by a feeling of awe and reverence, Ernie murmured, "I've never held a saint before."

For the first time in a long while, Jesse smiled. "Hold him tight then. We don't want him to escape."

Jesse took the statue from Ernie and, with his thumbs, applied gentle pressure against the plumed hat on the head of the saint. With great care, he removed the hat. Jesse turned the small piece of painted wood over in his hand.

"See that?"

"What? The only thing I see is a circle. Well," he said, as he leaned close to the wall to inspect the upside-down hat. "It looks like a plug in the bottom of the crown of the hat, sort of like a bottle cork."

"*Muy bien.* Remember Corey said there was something that would prove which was the real one, and that's why he knew the other was a fake?" asked Jesse.

"Didn't he say there was a curse on it?"

"Well, not exactly. It's not a curse on the statue but *in* the statue. Inside the hat, rolled up, is the curse. It is written on a piece of linen, like a scroll. It says that anyone who perturbs the statue will be cursed and those who venerate it will be blessed. Do you want me to take it out?" The haunted look in Jesse's eyes had vanished. His story had been vindicated.

Ernie shook his head. "*No es necesario.* You have convinced me, or maybe it was the Santo Niño I held who did it, that this is, *en verdad*, the original statue. We don't need to perturb it any more. Put it back where it was."

When the saint was safe in its special box, they placed it in the bag, and put it back in the space in the wall. Jesse pushed the rectangle back into the opening.

"It'll be safe here until the bishop comes."

They walked back to Ernie's truck together.

"What a story this will be to tell our descendants!" exclaimed Ernie.

"Yes, it's quite a story," replied Jesse with a grimace of wry humor. He knew the ending was not certain yet, not for Paco, not for Harold, not for himself. He hoped God would have mercy on them.

Their plan was to go to the Frontera Hospital. Jesse wanted to apologize and ask forgiveness before it was too late. But, always hungry, Ernie and Jesse stopped first at The Star for huge plates of enchiladas, a side of tamales, and a basket of *sopaipillas*.

When they arrived, Paco and Harold were outside the hospital waiting for them. They gave *abrazos* all around. They needed each other's strength.

"Guess what, Papi! Filomeno said something to me, but I could only understand part of it. I heard him say '*Ya me voy.*' I think he's going to die." Paco looked at his father.

"Did you tell him you were sorry?" Jesse asked. "What else did he say?"

When Paco tried to imitate what the phrase had sounded like, '*egote asolbo,*' both Ernie and Jesse understood the Latin phrase from their days as altar servers.

"*Dios mío,* Filomeno said he forgave you, in Latin, no less! That was buried deep in his brain! I can breathe again," Jesse exulted. Each one gave Paco a huge hug.

"I want to pay my respects," said Jesse. "Let's go."

They walked in together.

Beside Filomeno's bed, Jesse prayed as the others stood nearby.

"Bless us, O Lord, and all who honor the figure of the Christ Child, known as the Santo Niño de Atocha. We ask you, through His Blessed mother, Mary, to continue to protect our valley and all that lives within it. Forgive us, O Lord, for our pride, our selfishness, and our readiness to think ill of our brothers and sisters. Please allow Filomeno to return to us. We will care for him until the end of his days when You call him home. Help us support each other in caring for our families, our traditions, and our faith. Let us serve You faithfully so that we will see You face to face."

Así sea.

The Hidden Disclosed

Ernie carried the good news to Sara and Joshua that their authentic statue was safe. Those responsible for its disappearance had come forward and wanted to confess to the whole village. Sara immediately called the bishop and told him that their prayers had been answered. All the secrets of the Santo Niño's disappearance would be revealed.

The bishop agreed to come. He suggested that the people convene once again at the chapel in the village at noon on the next Saturday. He would bring Fr. Toledo with him. Word spread through the usual means. No one wanted to miss the historic occasion.

All ages came to hear the latest news, hunched *abuelitos* with their canes, tired housewives in simple dresses, dedicated members of the societies, workmen in stained Levis, a few young mothers with nursing babies. The people quieted, but someone whispered, "Look who decided to come."

Heads turned back toward the door and with surprise they watched Susana and David with his cane, accompany their mother, Rita, leaning on Jay's arm. He seated her, tipped his leather hat, and removed it when he sat down. His long legs stretched into the center aisle. He knows where he belongs, people whispered to each other and nodded with satisfaction.

On *La Nochebuena,* the faithful had celebrated the birth of the Christ Child in pageantry and ritual. When they kissed the tiny feet of the Baby Jesus, brought to the front of the altar from the manger during midnight Mass, they missed their little Santo Niño who was again hidden.

On Christmas Day afternoon, the *gente* used to visit their *vecinos* and their families. But today, few walked the paths from house to house. They went in pickup trucks or big heavy cars that had to be pushed when they got stuck in the snow or the mud. Usually both were abundant. At the neighbors' homes, the adults took a little sip or two of something warming that the young children were not allowed to drink. The youngsters were happy with *atole*, a sweetened corn-based drink, or hot chocolate made from scratch thickened with rich evaporated milk from a can.

But things were changing. Not so many people stayed home to receive their neighbors any more. More Anglos had moved in. Others had moved to town. The old ones rode in their grandsons' cars to join family in Peñasco, Española, El Rito, Albuquerque, Las Trampas, and Estancia. Their *hijitos* brought their Anglo girlfriends to introduce to the family. Young men and women with jobs often had to work on Christmas Day. On Christmas Day! What a travesty. The *abuelas* still made *empanadas* with spices, beef tongue and raisins in a rich crust, but today many of their sons and daughters brought store-bought goodies to family celebrations. Life changes, they said. *Así es la vida,* the elders sighed. The flow of life never freezes. It is like the river. It persists.

Those who remembered longed for the old days. On winter evenings, the nutty aroma of piñons in the oven roasting on a cookie sheet invited the family to gather to crack the tough shells to find the sweet kernels. It was a time for reminiscences, to tell stories of the *antepasados*, to pass along the latest news, and to remember the old days. In some homes, the rhythmic strumming on a guitar, accompanied perhaps by a fiddle, brought back the old days. Now the youngsters begged to watch TV and listen to their music instead of doing the "old-fashioned stuff."

At last the *vecinos* of Villa Vieja would hear why the statue had disappeared and who had taken it. The guilty were going to confess in front of the villagers. Everyone was anxious to discover the secrets. Nobody wanted to miss this meeting. It was better than the TV. Maybe peace would return to the valley.

Unaware of changes below the surface, even as melt water carved tunnels through the packed snow and etched its way through the ice that had hidden the truth, people felt the shift. The layers of tradition were cracking. Truth was leaking out. Soon, it would slide down the mountainside toppling trees, rearranging the terrain. The ice had cracked, but few heard it until they were once again summoned by the chapel bell to be witness, judge, and jury.

Holy Water Sprinkles

Bishop Kenney arrived dressed simply in black wearing a clerical collar and a simple stole with faint gold threads. He carried the crozier of a shepherd, but he did not wear his ecclesiastical ring. He eschewed forced obeisance and pomp. Fr. Toledo, however, in obsequious deference, opened the car door wide and gave the bishop his arm. The *mayordomos* greeted them and escorted them to seats in the front of the chapel.

When the bishop rose to speak, Fr. Toledo rushed to assist His Excellency by supporting his elbow as he ascended the steps of the raised wooden pulpit. The priest was determined to get back into His Grace's good graces.

Bishop Kenney looked down from the pulpit and smiled.

"My dear brothers and sisters, I come today to stand side-by-side with you to hear the last chapter of how the Santo Niño de Atocha statue was lost and now is found. For over one hundred years this image has lived in peace in Villa Vieja and remained safe from harm. Because of the unusual circumstance of its bestowal by the carver, Old Mister Benavídez, to the community, it became the patrimony of the *vecinos* of Villa Vieja.

"I was informed a few days ago that members of your own community have come forward with information about the disappearance and its whereabouts. They wish to confess to you all and ask for your forgiveness.

"Testimony will be presented by Jesse Fuentes, his son, Paco, and Rosie Dawn's son, Harold." Heads twisted as they looked around at their neighbors. I thought so. I knew it. They were up to no good.

"After that," continued Bishop Kenney, "here is how you will proceed. First, Officer Lucero will explain the criminal issues and possible legal consequences of their actions. Then those who are confessing will come forward. When the three have finished telling their stories, they will exit the chapel to await the results of your deliberations in the home of Sara and Joshua. You, as a community, must decide the just and proper course to take. Fr. Toledo and I will wait with them.

"As *vecinos,* you will deliberate on the degree of guilt or innocence of each person. Joshua will conduct the inquiry. Each person from the community has the right to speak. When you have finished your deliberations, we will return to hear the verdict.

"I will follow up with a letter that I will read at the next celebration of the Holy Eucharist here in your chapel on February 12, the feast of Our Lady of Lourdes. At that time, Corey has promised to explain to you, in detail, the story of the carver, Old Mister Benavídez, and the whole history of the carving of the statue.

"Because of your tenacious faith and devotion, I commend the people of Villa Vieja. You as a community have shown a spirit of solidarity and a desire to carry on the traditions and practices of the faith.

"The Church is composed of all its parts. There should be no separation between the people and the hierarchy. We are one as Christians. The only authority we follow is that of our Lord, Jesus Christ, the Savior. May you listen as Christ would. May you judge with the wisdom of Solomon. May God bless us all."

His Excellency raised his hand in blessing and left the chapel.

Joshua came forward and croaked in a hoarse voice that he was not able to lead the process. He suggested that, in his place, Jay be designated. He knew that Ernie had kept Jay informed of all that had occurred in the past few weeks. Jay agreed, as did the assembly by clapping their assent.

Jay stood before the people.

"*Hermanos y hermanas,* we are here to decide on several important questions: First, is the truth being told by each of the persons who will speak? Second, what punishment or forgiveness is due to each? Third, how may restitution to the community be made? Finally, is anyone from Villa Vieja willing to press charges on any or all of the three who will bear witness here? As Bishop Kenney urged us tonight, I repeat, 'May you listen as Christ would, and may you judge with the wisdom of Solomon.'"

Jay gave Ernie a thumb's up as he announced the next step.

"Detective Lucero has explained both the criminal and legal aspects to you. We will take thirty minutes for you to talk over these matters with your neighbors. Then, anyone who wants to come forward may rise and express her or his preferences or ask for clarification.

"My sister will write down in Spanish what you say. Rosie Dawn will take the statements in English. Both will read your comments back to you to make sure they are stated correctly. This will be your vote. Remember, you are weighing the truth of the witnesses, whether punishment or forgiveness is due, and what restitution must be made."

The process of deliberation was completed almost an hour later. The voices of multiple conversations had ascended to the roof dome where the two kneeling angels painted on the canopy still kept their peace.

Mando came to the front of the church.

Rosie gasped when she saw him.

"I know many of you are surprised to see me here," began Mando. "Let me say, simply, that people are capable of change. *Así es la vida.*" He glanced at Jay. "Thanks, bro."

Mando assumed his speech-making stance. He squared his shoulders and stood as tall as he could. "I was asked to report what you decided today. Here goes.

"The findings of the *gente* of Villa Vieja are the following: first, Jesse was the mastermind of the plan to take the original statue. You concluded that even though he went about it the wrong way, his purpose was to safeguard the statue, not exploit it. The bishop himself indicated that he understood that Jesse's motives were benign, not vicious. It was, in his words, 'misguided zeal.' However, he deceived the people and brought shame to the village because of jealousy and pride. Jesse also has suffered for the actions of his son, Paco. Nonetheless, Sara and Joshua have recommended Jesse to succeed them when they retire.

"As for Harold, he could have refused to deceive the people by making a copy of the statue, but he did not. In making the copy, he has shown so much talent that Corey has volunteered to teach him about religious art and carving, if he is serious about it."

Rosie bowed her head. Her long hair formed the curtain that masked her tears of relief. She could stay in Villa Vieja.

"Paco has had to face the possibility that his actions may have caused Filomeno irreparable harm. He must agree to learn to control his anger and take classes to do so. For restitution, as long as he lives in Villa Vieja, he will be the unpaid custodian of the chapel and will continue the work of his father with the *cofradía* in serving the needs of the less favored among us. If he wants to study criminal justice, Ernie has agreed to mentor him.

"Here is the most important consideration. When the three, accompanied by Ernie, paid a visit to Filomeno in the hospital, each one asked him for forgiveness. When Paco spoke, Filomeno opened his eyes and said, '*Ego te absolvo,*' and then he said, '*Ya me voy.*'"

Those who remembered their Latin gasped. Those who didn't inclined their heads and asked their neighbor what the words meant.

"For hundreds of years, the *vecinos* have protected their own. It was and is a matter of survival. The solidarity of the people remains strong. We follow this tradition even in today's world of change. We try to guide and help those who offend the community. Here is what you have decided: No one, *nadie*, not one single person, came forward to press charges. The drama is over, *punto.*" Mando stepped down from the altar step.

Applause and shouts of joy arose. *Abrazos* abounded.

Joshua and Sara rose and came forward together. Sara made the happy announcement.

"Remember, our original statue will be displayed again on the feast of Our Lady of Lourdes, when Bishop Kenney returns to celebrate the Mass with us. He will read a letter that will be of interest to everyone."

Joshua added, "After the Mass and before the fiesta begins, Corey has promised to tell us the whole story of Old Mister Benavídez, how he carved our statue, who made the curse, and how Corey proved the statue was a fake. So, that's it. *Vaya con Dios.*"

A Place to Rest

On February 12, Bishop Kenney read the following letter to the gathering in Villa Vieja:

"Greetings to the faithful of Villa Vieja, near Wild Turkey River, County of Saint Michael the Archangel. I begin with the words found hidden in the crown of the hat of the Santo Niño de Atocha carved in about 1870 by Benito Benavídez, *santero*:

> Blessed are they who love the Santo Niño de Atocha,
> But
> Cursed be they who maltreat his most holy image
> or perturb the place in which he rests.
> They shall suffer the fires of Hell for eternity.
> So be it.

"These words are part of your patrimony. Remember them and pass them on to the next generations so that your blessed statue may remain free from harm. Someone failed to pass on orally to this generation any knowledge of the curse. The archived records noted that this curse accompanies this statue. You have all suffered from this disgrace and felt that God had separated you from His protection. You must be diligent in your care for each other, for your families, for your traditions, and for your faith."

Many in the pews bowed their heads, ashamed. They felt that the bishop was castigating them.

"As some of you knew, the church leaders and I, with great regret, have been forced to close down a few of the mission chapels due to financial difficulties. This was a painful decision."

Ay, Dios, here comes the bad news.

"By Canon Law, all religious properties and structures belong to the bishop of the diocese. Therefore, I, Kenneth Alexander Kenney, Bishop of the diocese of the Holy Faith, publicly declare that the statue of the Santo Niño de Atocha will remain as the patrimony of the people of Villa Vieja forever. If, at some future time, another prelate should decide that the mission chapel be closed, I have officially created a space of honor for it in the cathedral. It would be removed from the village, but your statue would thus be available to your descendants and their descendants, *por los siglos.*"

As the meaning of the bishop's words became clear, applause erupted. It grew into cheers and then someone began a chant: "Viva el Santo Niño! Viva la Villa Vieja! Viva!"

Bishop Kenney smiled and made the Sign of the Cross over the assembly. "God bless you all. After Corey's *cuento*, it will be time to celebrate. "

Corey smiled at Bishop Kenney and began.

"As you know, every good story begins with the words, *Había una vez.* Here is the story of the *santero*, Old Mister Benavídez.

Once upon a time, over one hundred years ago, there was a *santero* named Benito Benavídez who lived in the village of Escondido.

As he did every morning, Old Mister Benavídez began early on his slow walk around the *sala* to greet the day. Benito, as he was known, enjoyed the cool, smooth feel of the packed earth floor beneath his stockinged feet. The image of his wife, Rebeca, hung the whitewashed wall, reminding him of his loss.

One *altarcito* held the images of the Sacred Heart and the Virgin de Guadalupe. His best friends were the saints who circled the room and called out to him. He greeted each statue briefly, noting the small crocheted circles that Rebeca had made to cover the top of each carved pedestal. Inclining before each one, Benito made his heartfelt requests for their blessings.

First, he prayed to San Francisco that he be able to show more kindness to all God's creatures, especially the difficult members of his family. Next, he appealed to *Nuestra Señora de Paz,* Our Lady of Peace, to curb his distrust of his fellow villagers.

Lastly, he beseeched San Isidro the Worker, patron of the fields, that his corn, beans, fruits and flowers would grow well this year in the small plot behind his house. Beside each one, he lit a votive candle in a colored glass cup. A few dried flowers accented each saint's own special space. In the dim light, the low relief carvings, los *retablos*, looked almost alive.

When he finished his rounds, he felt a halo of protection around him. In his workshop, Benito had a rickety table upon which he saved broken pieces of his carvings. He and Rebeca had called it the "table of damaged saints." Today he smiled at the memory of how the two of them had laughed at the phrase. Sometimes, memories of his wife brought a hint of tears to his slightly bloodshot eyes. That's what we all are, he mused, damaged saints.

From boyhood, Benito had been devoted to certain saints. They became as familiar to him as his own grandfathers and grandmothers, aunts and uncles. He listened to them, scolded them, ignored their implorations, and thanked them. It depended on the day. Since the personages they represented had been friends of Our Lord's in life, he trusted them. He prayed for their strong spirits to guide him. Now that he was a widower, he conversed with them more often.

After he completed the circuit of saints, he put on his old leather shoes, picked up a small basket and went out the back door. The brightly lit garden looked healthier since the rains, he noted with pleasure. Benito enjoyed the gaiety of the bold sunflowers, the tall hollyhocks standing guard above the smaller flowers in tin cans that bloomed near the rich chocolate of the adobe walls. Benito carefully tended the flowers he had transplanted from the mountainside, purple asters, blue and yellow columbines. Feathery cosmos in orange and pink opened flower faces that seemed to smile at him. He smiled back. He was especially proud that the wild roses he had transplanted grew well. In the fall, he would gather up the rose hips and make a healthy tea to sustain him through the winter. His raspberries had also thrived, and a few were ripe. He smiled as he savored each tiny scarlet gem that juiced his tongue.

Next, Benito strewed dried corn for the chickens, gathered a few speckled eggs, and picked a ripe peach for lunch. After he had prepared his usual breakfast of fried eggs liberally doused with green chile, *papas fritas,* and a couple of corn tortillas that one of the ladies in the village made for him, he gulped a cup of strong coffee and readied himself. Today was a special day and he had no time to dawdle. At last, he was going to begin the carving of the Holy Child, the Santo Niño.

Although the Santo Niño was one of his favorites, Benito had long felt intimidated by the complexity of the image. Benito was a good craftsman, but he was self-taught. El Niño had daunted him because of the two separate carved elements, the chair or throne, and the figure itself. Never had he carved a seated figure in a chair. But arthritis was beginning to stiffen his fingers and his hands were not as dexterous as before. He knew he had to begin the carving while he was still could.

Benito tried to visualize the few images he had seen of the Holy Child. They usually presented him as a chubby-faced youth seated in a throne-like chair wearing a wide-brimmed hat from which sprouted a flourish of feathers. Around his neck, a huge white ruffled collar suggested a Spanish grandee. Below a pair of puffy knee breeches, white stockings warmed his plump legs. Sandals bared his toes. The young pilgrim always grasped a staff in one hand from which dangled one or two gourds filled with water for the journey and he carried a basket of bread loaves or, in other images, a basket of roses. Engravings Benito had seen of El Niño showed a gold scallop shell pinned to his jacket, but since there were no seashells around his mountains, he decided to leave out that detail. This somewhat fussy dandy was not how Benito imagined his carving of El Niño Jesus.

Benito had wondered about this Christ Child. How could this young person be the poor Child born in a stable with the animals? If the Holy Child were a Spanish pilgrim, shouldn't He be standing or striding? Why was He always resting? He often looked more like a prince than a pilgrim. His carving would show other aspects of the spirit of the Holy Child.

Turning his thoughts to the carving, Benito tried to see in his mind how to design the figure and the chair it sat in. I have never made a seated figure before. Should it be all carved from one piece of wood? What if I make a mistake or use the wrong symbols? Never mind. When the priest comes to say Mass the next time, I'll ask him which symbols to use and why they matter. In the tiny hamlet in the northern part of *Nuevo España,* Benito might wait months, even years, for a priest's visit. He knew he couldn't put off carving the saint any longer. No one knew how much time was allotted for his or her stay on this *santa tierra*, this holy earth. He could ask the priest later.

Benito went out to a small storage room near the chicken coop that he shared with a few mice, several species of spiders, an occasional pack rat, and many little flying bothers. The small room had an old flat roof of long *vigas*, stripped logs of pine. Cross pieces, *latillas*, formed simple diagonals between the logs. Above the structure, melted adobes provided soil from which in summer grasses grew. Benito used to let his goats out of their pens to graze on the roof. Their sharp hooves packed the soil. When it rained, the water left standing in the corners began to melt the adobe wall below. The roof was like him, he admitted, getting old, weakened and leaky. Neither going to last long.

A battered table, deeply gouged, stood along one wall. Along the cuts, layers of different colors of paint revealed its age. A tiny window admitted a limited amount of light through a slice of mica that filled the small frame. When it was warm outside, Benito left the door open for more air. Scraps of wood, half-cut logs, table legs, broken chairs and unfinished projects filled the cobwebbed corners of his tiny workshop.

Benito was a *carpintero* who made furniture to sell or trade with his neighbors. He liked the fact that *Jesúcristo*, and his foster father, *San José*, were carpenters. He felt a physical and spiritual kinship with them when he worked. Carpenters spoke the language of the hands, he thought, of skill and service. Benito was proud of his work. Each time he began a new carving, he asked the saints to guide his knife and keep him on the right path.

After a brief prayer, Benito groaned a little, straightened his bent back, gathered his tools and his energy, and sighed. He began sketching with a piece of coal that he found near the woodpile in back. When he made a sketch of both figure and chair together, it looked awkward. The top of the chair seemed to be sprouting from the Child's shoulders and His body was suspended above the seat. So Benito decided to make the carving in two separate parts, the figure of the Holy Child and the throne. Benito felt relieved. He would have time in the winter to think about how to join the two parts into a whole.

After the cold settled in, he would invite all of his unfinished saints into the big room, the *sala*. His wife had built the cozy rounded corner fireplace that provided him warmth. On the ledge in front of the fire, he sometimes placed pieces of wood to dry. Above the small stone mantel, Benito had made an oval niche in which his newly completed saint would rest. For now, he had placed a candle there, holding the space for the statue until he finished the Santo Niño. But now, it was summer, and he could work in his workshop. He had plenty to do if the Holy Child were to be completed by Christmas.

Benito followed the customs of other *santeros* as he prepared himself for his new project. For three days prior to beginning, he fasted, according to his own fashion. He drank only one cup of black coffee instead of three, ate a hard-boiled egg sprinkled with salt, and one *tortilla* spread with refried beans for breakfast. For snacks, he ate only apples or dried peaches. For dinner, he skipped the *papas* and ate greens from his garden alongside a large pork chop made from his last pig killed at its *matanza* the year before. He prayed to all his favorite saints and threw in a couple of prayers to the Virgin of Guadalupe and Our Lady of Peace, as well. With their help, he could make a saint that would aid people in the practice of their faith. Old Mister knew how hard it was to stay on the right path. He had stumbled more than once. He hoped his devotion would make up for his transgressions.

Making a saint demanded prayer and concentration. One almost had to be a saint to carve a saint. Benito knew he was no saint, but he depended on the loving forgiveness of the Holy Child. He often thought of Christ's sufferings as he carved – the cruel cuts made by the scourging, the tearing of the forehead by the crown of thorns, the deep wound from the Roman lance thrust into His side while He hung on the cross. As he worked, he felt at one with the sufferings of Christ and the saints.

Benito made most of the tools he used from scrap metal or bone he found in the forest. Sometimes it took almost as long to fashion a new tool as it did to carve the piece. He followed his usual plan. He carved the *corpus*, the body, and then shaped the head, the arms and legs. The special attributes of each saint, such as a fish, a skull, a plow, a dragon, a basket, or a staff, Benito whittled with special care. For the Santo Niño, however, he also had to carve a wide-brimmed hat on the Child's head and make long, delicate, feathery plumes. This Santo Niño was a saint with flair, with *penache*. After he had carved the pieces, he joined them to the *corpus* either with glue he made from boiling hooves or attached a small piece of tanned leather that allowed the arm or leg to move and bend. Once he rounded and shaped the pieces, he rubbed them with pumice stone to smooth them. Finally, he coated the wood with *gesso*. When dry, the surface absorbed the colors of the pigments he himself made from elements in the stones. Benito lifted a piece of cottonwood, held it up to the light, noted the indentations and protuberances of the wood, crossed himself, and began.

A knock on the outside of the workshop startled him. His face contracted like a dried plum. I do not need checking on by this bothersome *viejita*, he muttered, as he stuck his head out of the low doorway. He knew she would persist until he gave in. Better to get it over with now.

"Who's there?" he shouted, irritated at the intrusion.

"It's Doña Eloisa, *viejito*, your neighbor."

"What do you want this time?"

"I brought you some fresh tortillas, and I just wanted to check on you."

"Can't you see I'm working? Come back later." Benito put down the cottonwood root.

A small-boned figure with wrinkled face and a young girl's body waited near the door.

"Ay, Benito, how you treat your friends! I won't take long."

"*Bueno, aquí estoy.* Here I am. *¿Qué quieres?*" She always wanted something from him.

Over the years, Doña Eloisa had heard many stories about the irascibility of her best friend's husband, but his wife, Rebeca, insisted that he had a good heart.

As the village midwife, Doña Eloisa had seen both the bright and dark sides of her neighbors. She shared the pangs of labor with her clients as well as the joy of bringing out a healthy child. When the results were sad, she shared their grief. She rejoiced with them at a healthy baby. She had learned to use her herbs to treat her neighbors' complaints, from headaches to broken bones, to *El Ojo*, the evil eye. Doña Eloisa knew everyone in their tiny cluster of houses attached to the side of the mountain, and, like Benito, trusted few. She had seen firsthand how pain and *envidia* made people vulnerable, how they lashed out with unkind acts.

"Here are some tortillas," she said as she handed him the dish-towel covered plate. "I made them this morning. What are you doing in that little shack?"

"It's none of your business, but since you asked, I am going to carve a new *bulto*. I was just about to start when you interrupted me."

"Which one this time? Did someone ask for it? Did the priest commission it? Is it for our church here? I thought you weren't going to carve anymore."

"*Ay, mujer.* How many questions can you rattle off in one breath?"

"Well, at least tell me which saint it's going to be."

"This one is the Santo Niño. I don't know what will happen to it. I am making it for myself this time."

"People will talk. *Ay,* you know how they are. You're not supposed to make *santos* for yourself. People will say what's Benito up to? Who does he think he is? Maybe some will say you're the least saintly person they know. Maybe they will say about you what they say about me. They'll think you are a *brujo*. Be prepared, *viejo.*"

"*¡Al infierno con todos ellos!* To hell with them! I'll show them." He paused for moment as a devious idea came to him. His glare lessened and a gleam showed in his eyes.

"Doña Eloisa, maybe you can help me. You know about blessings and curses. What if I put a curse on anyone who tampers with the statue? That would fix them."

Benito did not trust people easily. He was convinced his neighbors were stealing from him. His best hammer was missing, some boards he had piled in the back were gone, and his pet goat had disappeared – into someone's kettle or cooking pot, he suspected.

"Ah, so now you need my help. How about thanks for the *tortillas* first?"

Benito bowed deeply and, with a sweeping gesture, he pretended to remove his non-existent hat.

"Thank you so much for the delicious tortillas, most gracious lady. I am much obliged to you," he said.

"Don't be sarcastic to me, you old fool. Besides, what you are asking is dangerous. God will not like that."

"He knows how bad his children are. It's for the protection of the little saint itself and the people who love him."

"I don't know...."

"Think about how to make a good curse on a thief. I have to get to work. *Adios.* Benito turned his back and went toward his workshop.

"*Vaya con Dios* or else you will be walking with the Devil, Benito."

"Don't forget what I said."

"You, too." Doña Eloisa let herself out into the warmth and peace of a late summer day.

Several weeks passed without any perturbations, and Benito began his carving. When the day was pleasant, he worked outside. When he stretched his shoulders and looked out, he saw that clouds had started to pile up in fluffy blue-white heaps over the crest of the mountains. Better move inside to his workshop, just in case of a sudden thunderstorm. He gathered up his tools and covered his worktable with sheets of rusty tin and weighted them down with large rocks he found lying around. As he picked up the partially shaped left arm of the saint, he heard someone coming along the rocky path that led to his house. He hoped whoever it was would go away. Big drops began to fall as he heard a voice.

"Benito, I have fresh tortillas for you."

He knew that voice. Since it had started to rain, hospitality demanded that he invite his guest into his small kitchen. He put the chipped white enamel coffee pot on the wood stove. This time, he wanted to talk. Eloisa was one of the few women who could read and write. She knew big words to use when she made up the prayers she said over her patients. Like him, Doña Eloisa also had the spice of mischief and a bit of distrust in her neighbors.

"Come in. Let's see how good your tortillas are this time."

Doña Eloisa shook off a few raindrops, removed her heavy woven jacket, and sat her petite body down on a sturdy wooden chair at the kitchen table covered with oilcloth.

"So, how are you?" she asked brightly.

"Not too bad, considering. How about some coffee?"

"*Gracias.* I got cold when the rain started." Eloisa covered her mouth and stifled a cough.

Benito peeked under the cloth that covered the tortillas and the aroma made him smile.

"Ah, these tortillas are still warm. Let's have some."

Benito went to the *trastero,* the wooden cupboard he had made, and removed a pot of the raspberry jam. He put it on the table and laid a battered metal spoon beside it. He removed two chipped blue enamel plates and set them down. He was not used to having someone at his table, but he needed her help.

"How is the statue coming along?"

"I am making progress slowly."

"Can I see it?"

"No! Not yet. I don't let anyone see my work until I finish it." Benito gave her such a look that Eloisa grew quiet. "Any news of the neighbors?"

She was surprised that Benito had asked. "Not much. No babies to deliver and no really sick people right now, so that's good, *gracias a Dios.* I am not so busy these days."

"Doña Eloisa, remember what we talked about before?"

Eloisa nodded her head carefully wondering where this was going to lead.

"I have thought about this a lot. If the rumor of a curse accompanies the image as it is passed down to the next generations, the statue would be more protected, *qué no?* No one would dare tamper with it or harm it. It would be revered by many people."

What he did not tell her about was the little voice in the back of his mind that whispered that the *santero* might be honored, too.

"As I told you before, the people won't like it."

"Maybe they don't have to know. You and I will know. When I die, make sure my sons give the Niño to the little village in the river valley across the mountain. Mention that there is a curse on the statue for anyone who disrespects it. Only the *mayordomos* need to know. They can use this information if they need to."

"Why there?"

"I made a *promesa* to Rebeca, my wife, that I would do this. Villa Vieja is the village where she was born. I want it to stay there for our descendants. I need your help."

Doña Eloisa bowed her head as she remembered Rebeca. They had shared many confidences and giggled like school girls over the smallest things. She considered Benito's words. Although Old Mister Benavídez, as the younger ones called him now, was hard to get along with, he had a good heart, just as Rebeca had told her.

"What do you do you need from me?"

"I will hollow out a small compartment inside the statue. Then you and I will compose a curse. You know some fancy words. I can't write, but you can, thanks to your father. You will write the curse very small on a tiny piece of linen. Roll it up like a scroll and we will put it inside."

Benito was out of practice at being diplomatic and persuasive. He hoped Doña Eloisa had understood him. He did not like to ask for help. Both were quiet and they said their goodbyes.

After about two weeks, Doña Eloisa returned and showed him what she had written. After a few disagreements about the wording, they felt they had an effective curse.

> *Benditos sean todos ellos que aman al Santo Niño de Atocha*
> *Pero*
> *Maldito sea alguién que maltrata*
> *su santísima imagen*
> *o perturba el nicho en que El descansa*
> *Que ellos sufran los fuegos del infierno*
> *para siempre.*
> *Así sea.*

"When I am ready to put the curse in the carving, I will let you know, *si quiera?*"

"Yes, I want to see how you do it. We both better pray for forgiveness."

"Don't worry so much. It's a good thing. It will keep the image safe."

Several months later, Benito sent word to Eloisa to come by. He had the carving on the kitchen table.

"Oh Benito, it is so cunning. I want to pick up and rock the Child." She was amazed at how well he had captured the sweet saint's appeal. She neared the table.

"Don't touch it," he yelled. "The glue's not dry."

Later, after they drank their coffee, Benito showed her the tiny compartment he had hollowed out in the crown of the plumed hat. They put the rolled linen scroll inscribed with the curse into it with great care. They pressed the small wooden plug tight. Benito took a tiny brush and dipped it into the varnish he had made and sealed the entire opening. He put it in the window sill where the late afternoon's rays were slanting their blessed golden light into the kitchen.

"The hiding place will not be noticed. Remember, the purpose of the curse is to protect the statue from harm, not only to punish los *malvados.*"

With a serene smile, Benito went to the *trastero* and brought out two glasses and a bottle of peach wine he had received in exchange for a small carved chest he had made for the birth of someone's grandson. He set the glasses on the table, filled them each half-full, and looked gratefully at his friend.

"We did it," he toasted her. "We have made sure that no one will ever molest this statue. "*Salud,*" Benito smiled as he and Eloisa clinked their glasses and sipped the fragrant nectar.

"May God bless us and not curse us, Benito." She raised her precise eyebrows and winked at him.

After she left, Benito resumed work in a frame of mind that, for him, was almost euphoric. He began humming off-key as he picked up his tools to finish the last details of his Santo Niño de Atocha.

"And that is how the story ends, the true story of your statue. Now, we have some celebrating to do." Corey received loud applause for his telling of the history of the carving and the curse.

As the clapping ceased, someone yelled out, "How do you know this? Maybe you just made up that whole story."

Corey explained, "I found the account in the state archives. Doña Eloisa was one of a few women in the area who could read and write in Spanish. Her journals were found when she died. She had kept careful records of births, deaths and other significant events in Escondido in her journal. Her family donated them to the state archives, and they are preserved for future generations."

Applause silenced the cynic.

Mending the Colcha

"Let's celebrate our blessings!" Corey extended his hands to the heavens.

The sapphire air of February was crisp and cold. The musicians began tuning up their instruments, and several wished they had their gloves. But they would sacrifice a little comfort to make the celebration festive. Sounds of guitars, fiddles, a flute, and even a trumpet, competed, an assault on the ears until they melded into the familiar rhythms the villagers had known and danced to since childhood. The ladies brought platters and pots filled with tamales, enchiladas, rice, beans, chile con carne, and posole. The aroma of fresh tortillas warmed nostrils and hearts. The wooden table held bowls of chile con carne, chicken in a thick, rich sauce called *mole*, and carne asada. The smell of roasted pork was inviting. Cakes, fruit pies and Jell-O in bright clear colors in plastic cups attracted longing looks. Today the *gente* joined together in their rejoicing as they had in their suffering.

When the village boys and girls, who had been playing tag, saw Paco heading for a large cottonwood with a rope and a *piñata*, they swarmed like a flock of starlings and ran after him toward the river.

An unfamiliar car crawled slowly toward the adults who stood in clusters, talking and shaking their heads at the events of the past year. When they heard the low growl of the motor, the *gente* knew they were strangers. Party crashers were not common in their high valley. All eyes watched as the big Buick pulled onto the gravel skirt and parked.

The door opened and the driver, a middle-aged man with slicked-back, black hair got out and stretched his arms and shook out his shoulders. A woman in her thirties, dressed modestly in a long beige skirt and sweater set, wore a knit cap and a green coat. She opened the back door on the passenger's side. Two young boys, dressed in long pants and warm denim jackets descended reluctantly from the car. One rounded the back of the car and caught sight of Jay.

"*¡Hóla! Señor* Sierra. We're here!" Ramón ran toward Jay.

Jay loped toward him and knelt down to give Ramón a hug. His little brother, Pablo, had short, chubby legs and didn't run as fast. When he reached Jay, he jumped onto his knee. All three squeezed each other tightly.

Some of the villagers turned with expressions of surprise. Several lifted eyebrows and wondered if Jay had his own secrets. Was it possible the boys were his?

Jay got up and shook hands with the couple. "*Bienvenidos.* I'm glad you came. Let me introduce you to my friends and family."

Jay clapped his hands and banged on the table to get their attention.

"*Mis amigos*, this is *Señor* Miguel Romero and his wife, Luisa, who drove all the way from Tres Cruces. I invited them. Please welcome them as you do my family."

Several people stepped forward to shake the hands of these newcomers, including Ernie and his two sons who had been helping carry Cokes and Nehi grape soda to the drinks table. The boys watched each other without a word. Then Ernie's older son, Vicente, said, "Come on. There's going to be a *piñata*. Maybe we'll break it and get the candy. *¡Vámonos!*" The four ran across the meadow. Ernie was proud his son had welcomed the newcomers.

"It looks like the boys have made friends," Ernie observed. "*Bueno*, so what's the story, *amigo*? Everyone wants to know. Did you have a friend down south when you were in college you never told me about?" He winked and raised a quizzical eyebrow. Maybe now he would find out why Jay had been so evasive.

Jay hesitated. "Can you keep this under your hat – like the Santo Niño?"

Ernie nodded.

"OK, I'll tell you, just you, but no one else. Tell the others the Romeros are just friends from Tres Cruces, *no más*. I don't want anybody else to know, understand, no one. You got it?" Jay's piercing green-gold eyes glittered.

Ernie turned his palms upward *"Claro que sí.* Go on."

Jay nodded. "One day I was called to translate for a case in Family Court. I learned that these boys had been abandoned by their parents who were involved in heavy drugs, and then the parents were killed. Ramón and Pablo had no one. They spoke no English, and they were scared. I know how it is to lose a parent, or both, so I asked for temporary custody and got it. I hired Luisa to come in during the day to watch them. They were with me for about four months. They needed an adult they could trust. They're great little kids. Now Luisa and Miguel want to adopt them. Do you see why I couldn't just leave every time you called?"

When Jay paused, he and Ernie looked across the field and saw all four boys talking and jumping with excitement as they took turns swinging the stick at the colorful *piñata* dangling from a low cottonwood branch. Contentment warmed the chilly afternoon.

Jay went on. "I want the boys to come visit Villa Vieja when they can," Jay continued. "I see they already have two friends." Jay felt his eyes filling up.

"What? You're coming home?" asked Ernie.

"Just as soon as I can figure out how – this is where I belong. The Romeros want to adopt the boys. It may take a while, but they'll have a home. That's it. Don't make a big deal out of it. You promised not to tell. *En boca cerrada no entran moscas,* remember?"

Ernie gave Jay the high sign. Another reason to celebrate.

In high spirits, all who had taken a part in solving the secret of the plumed saint gathered in groups to rehash the incredible story of the statue's disappearance. Even those who had suspected each other forgot their grievances.

"I feel really proud of the *gente*," said Jay. "We stuck together."

"Yeah, and look at the ones who confessed. The community didn't kick them out. They embraced them. Maybe this brought some good in the long run," said Ernie as he turned to Jay.

"Did you hear about Mando?" asked Rosie. "He got a part-time job in town with an agency that fights for workers' rights. He can continue his work for the *raza* that he started in California." Jay was surprised to hear that Mando and Rosie had already spoken.

When Jesse came over to them, each one embraced him. "I cannot believe that the *gente* has forgiven me. By the way, Paco already has gone for counseling on anger management. And he's eating everything in sight. I have my son back." They noticed how suffering had aged Jesse. There were grey hairs among the russet ones that coiled from under his cap.

Rosie looked at them all together, a team, and said, "Imagine, my *hito* could even become a *santero*," she smiled," but probably not a *santo*." They all laughed.

When La Doña approached with Mando, Rosie held her breath. They greeted each other politely. Mando remained quiet as she addressed Rosie and the others.

"Now that the truth is known, we can all go back to our regular routines." Doña Amargarita announced. Then she looked straight at Rosie, who did not blink, and spoke. "I am getting old and need a helper to gather herbs and to learn about how to use them. I have seen that you have a way with plants. I'd like for you to help me."

Mando smiled when he heard Rosie's response, her face as rosy as her name.

"I would be honored to work with you, Doña Amargarita. When would we start?"

"In early spring. Only *locos* would go now," she retorted with her usual sharpness. At this, she was hailed by someone and ambled over to find out the latest *mitote*.

In Villa Vieja, villagers who had been suspicious and unkind to each other examined their own consciences. The statute's disappearance had tested their strengths and revealed their weaknesses. With new appreciation, they recalled what the old ones had told them:

Hold on to each other and your families.
Support your *vecinos* with kindness.

Do not be afraid to show repentance and ask for forgiveness.
Remain loyal to the community.
If one of you is weak, help strengthen her or him.
Repair the solidarity of the community as you would a torn *colcha*.
Mend a few threads at a time.

The fiesta finally broke up in the late afternoon. As the people of Villa Vieja made their way home, the setting sun filled the sky with luscious, peach clouds. A coral haze lingered in the air softening the contours of their beloved valley into a luminous landscape worthy of a Peter Hurd painting.

In March, Dr. Parkhurst advised the village that he would like to buy the replica made by Harold and Paco for $2,000. He planned to donate it to the Frontera University Fine Arts Department to demonstrate the current use of traditional materials and carving techniques. Harold and Paco each received $500. The rest of the money went to the chapel for upkeep and improved security.

By April, Filomeno had regained consciousness and was permitted to leave the hospital but he was no longer able to live alone. As they had promised, Jesse and Paco took the frail sacristan into their home. Every morning Filomeno gave thanks for the blessing of his new family who would care for him to the end. The old sacristan sat on the porch in the sun and looked out upon the valley he had loved for more than 70 years. When neighbors brought in food, they talked about the old days. Filomeno was content. The valley came back to life. Families cleansed the *acequias* and readied the fields for planting. Spring green lit the trees with hope for new beginnings and a good year.

In May, Filomeno passed on. The hospital report showed he died of a heart attack unrelated to the injuries he had sustained.

Filomeno joined Old Mister Benavídez. As the two looked down on their Villa Vieja, a honey-colored haze hovered above the high mountain valley. They saw that the river still gleamed and dark pines pointed to the sky. Light, like a blessing, lingered in the village.

The *gente* would continue to survive.

"I guess that curse Doña Eloisa and I made saved your Santo Niño, after all," remarked the *santero*.

The old men chuckled.

The End

Glossary

The northern New Mexico dialect is referred to by linguists as the Rio Arriba dialect. Code-mixing of Spanish and English terms is characteristic of the area. The glossary provides equivalents for expressions in Spanish in the sense used in the story. It omits common words borrowed from Spanish into English, such as plaza, adobe, pronto, fiesta, and common food items. Less familiar terms for food from northern New Mexico are included. Latin words crucial to the story are translated. The French word, *penache*, is defined by its expanded meaning in English.

Abrazo Hug, embrace
Abrumado Crushed, overwhelmed
Abuelitos Grandparents
Acequia Irrigation ditch
Ahora Now, right now
¡Al infierno con todos ellos! To Hell with all of them!
Alabados Old Spanish hymns
Altarcito Small altar or shrine, often in a home
Amigo(a) Friend
Anglo Caucasian, White, non-Hispanic
Animalitos Little carved animals
Antepasados Ancestors
Aquí estoy Here I am
Así es That's how it is
Así es la vida That's life
Así sea So be it. Amen
Atole Drink made with corn meal and sweetened

I

Ay, que triste Oh, how sad

Barrio Slum, poor neighborhood

¡Basta! Enough!

Bienvenido Welcome

Bolo Tie slide with simple piece of jewelry, worn by men

Brujo(a) Witch, sorcerer, male or female

Buena gente A good person

Buenas noches Good evening

Bueno Good, OK, well

Bueno, aquí estoy OK, here I am

Bueno, bye Code mix of Spanish and English, indicates end of conversation

Bulto Three-dimensional image of saint or Holy Family carved and painted

Café con leche Coffee with cream, light-skinned

Campesino Field worker, usually impoverished

Camposantos Burial grounds, cemeteries

Capilla Chapel, mission chapel

Carnal Affectionate term between males, blood brother

Casita Small house, usually modest

Chicanos(as) Term for Hispanos, short for Mexicans, associated with political activism

Chicos Kernels of dried roasted corn used in stews

Chiquitos(as) Little ones, children

Cilantro A variety of parsley

Claro Sure

Claro que sí Of course

Cofradía Organization that serves social and religious needs of a community

Comité Group selected to perform a special task

Como la gente Like one of us

Compa' Abbreviation for companion, buddy, friend

Con su permiso With your permission, allow me

Conquistador Conqueror

Corpus Latin for figure or body

Coyote Person who is mixed, Hispano and Caucasian; common canine in Southwest

Cuento de hadas Fairy tale

Cuídate   Take care of yourself, be careful
Curandera   Healer, herbalist, medicine woman
Desafortunadamente   Unfortunately
Desgracia   Disgrace, embarrassment
Dicho   Spanish saying
Dígame   Tell me
Dios mío   My God
Dios te bendiga   God bless you
Don, Doña   Titles of respect, male, female
Duerme con los angelitos   Bedtime blessing, lit., sleep with the little angels
Educación   Upbringing, manners
Egote asolbo   Corruption of Latin phrase
Ego te absolvo   Latin for I forgive you
El Ojo   The evil eye
El santo emplumado   The plumed saint
Empanadas   Fried or baked spiced meat pies
En boca cerrada no entran moscas   Keep your mouth shut, it's secret, don't tell.
En mi casa   At my house, in my house
En verdad   In truth, really
Enojado   Upset, irritated
Envidia   Envy, jealousy
Ermitaño   Hermit of Pilgrim's Peak
Es algo muy malo   It's something very bad
Es como una fábula   It seems like a fable
Ese   Slang term used by males
Es tarde   It's late
Espantajo   Scarecrow
Estoy contento   I am happy, content
Fíjate   Imagine, imagine that
Fue mi orgullo   It was my pride
Gente   People of the village, (my) people, the people
Gesso   Mixture of gypsum and animal glue applied to statues prior to painting
Girasoles   Sunflowers
Gracias   Thanks
Gracias a Dios   Thank God

Gringos Caucasians, light-skinned, sometimes called *Americanos*
Güeros Blond, fair-skinned people
Hasta Later
Hasta mañana See you tomorrow
Había una vez Once upon a time
Hermano mayor Religious leader, lit., older brother
Hermanos y hermanas Ladies and gentlemen, brothers and sisters
Hijito(a) Term of endearment for boys or girls
Hijo(a) Son, daughter
¡Hóla! Greeting, Hello, Hi there
Hombre Man
Honcho Big man, leader, boss
Igualmente The same to you
Jefe, jefa Boss
Kachinas Images of spirits or gods, Native American
La Doña Boss lady, uncomplimentary, used with irony
La Llorona Woman of legend who laments for her lost children along river banks
La Nochebuena Christmas Eve
La raza Identity marker used by Hispanos to mean my people
La raza cósmica Mixture of European and native peoples of the Americas
Las Posadas A drama before Christmas in which Mary and Joseph seek shelter
La verdad The truth
Las razas Ethnicities, races
Latillas Small wooden slats
Loca Crazy woman
Malas noticias Bad news
Malvados Trouble-makers
Mamá Mother, mom
'Mano(a) Abbreviation, term of endearment for brother or sister
Más Very, more
Matanza Killing of a pig with associated activities followed by a feast
Mayordomos Caretakers, persons responsible for special duties
Me voy I'm going
Mestizaje Mixture of ethnicities

Mexicano Mexican
Mezcla A mix, as in vegetables in a salad
Mi'jo(a) My son or my daughter
Mitote Gossip
Mitotera One who gossips
Mojados Derogatory term, slang for wetbacks, undocumented workers
Morada A meeting house for religious activities
Mota Code word for marijuana
Mucho dinero Lots of money
Mujer Woman, wife
Muy buena gente Good person
Muy exigente Very strict
Muy frío Cold-hearted
Muy guapo Very handsome
Muy inteligente Very smart
Nada Nothing
Nadie No one
Negocio(s) Business, matters to discuss
Ni una palabra Not a word
No más No more
No sé I don't know
No te preocupes Don't worry about it
Noticias News, information
Nueva España New Spain, territory colonized by Spain
¡!Ojalá que sí I hope so
¡Ojalá! I hope, if only, God willing (from Arabic: Allah)
Ojos Eyes, springs of water
Orgullo Pride
Otra vez Again, once more
Padre Biological father, priest
Padre Title as form of address for clerics
Panza Belly
Papá Father, dad
Papas fritas Fried potatoes
Papi Daddy
Partera Midwife
Pásale Come in

Patrimonio   Patrimony, legacy, heritage
Pecadillo   Minor fault, minor sin
Penache   French for feather or plume, stylish, with a flourish
Pendejo   Jerk, bastard, SOB
Perdóname   Excuse me
Piñata   Decorated container with candy for children to break with stick at birthdays, celebrations
Piñón   Evergreen which produces nuts used as a food item
Piñones   Sweet pine nuts
Pobrecito(a)   Someone who suffers, is poor, someone to be pitied
Pobrecitos(as)   Less fortunate ones
Policía   Police
Políticos   Politicians
Por favor   Please
Por los siglos   Forever
¿Por qué?   Why?
Portal   Entry, porch
Porvenir   The future, what is to come
Posole   Stew made with meat, parched corn, onions, cumin, garlic and chile
Pues   Time-filler in speech, um, well
Punto   Period, the end
¿Qué es esto?   What's that?
¡Qué lástima!   What a pity
¡Qué mariquita!   What a sissy!
¿Qué no?   Don't you think?
¡Qué Satanás!   What a Devil!
¿Qué sé yo?   What do I know? How would I know?
¿Quién está?   Who's there?
¿Quién sabe?   Who knows?
Rancheras   Popular songs in Spanish
Remedios   Remedies, medicines
Retablo   Religious painting on a flat pine board hung on the wall
Rezador   Leader of prayers
Rosita querida   Dear Rosie
Sala   Living room
Salchicha   Sausage
Salsa   Sauce, gravy

Salud Cheers, to your health
San José Saint Joseph
Santa tierra Holy ground, sacred earth
Santero Carver of religious art
Santo Niño de Atocha Holy Child (Christ Child) of Atocha
Señor(a) Mister, Mrs., title of respect
Señor, ten piedad de nosotros Lord, have mercy on us
Señoritas Young ladies
Si quieres If you want to, as you wish
Sí, se puede Yes, we can. Rallying cry of Chicano activist César Chavez
Sopaipillas Puffed, fried dough in the shape of little pillows
Tiempos pasados Times past, the old days
Tío(a) Uncle, aunt
Trastero Cupboard, sideboard (Río Arriba dialect)
Vámonos Let's go
¡Vamos a luchar! Let's fight!
Vatos locos Bad guys, trouble-makers
Vaya con Dios God bless you, lit., go with God
Vecinos Neighbors
Vegas Meadows
Vergüenza Shame or embarrassment
Viejo(a) Old
Viejitos(as) Old ones, the elderly
Vigas Wooden crossbeams
Yerba buena Mint tea

Discussion Guide

1. Which character in *The Secrets of the Plumed Saint* intrigued you the most and why? What are your judgments about this character, positive and negative?

2. Why is the disappearance of the statue of the Santo Niño so important to the community of Villa Vieja? What reasons do the villagers give for its loss?

3. The setting of Villa Vieja in a high mountain valley affects the villagers' lifestyle in a number of ways. Living in view of Pilgrim's Peak, for example, serves as a mnemonic of the hermit's life of dedication. Have you ever lived in a place where natural forces and landmarks had a strong effect on your routines, career choices, and physical and/or spiritual well-being?

4. Nearly all the characters rely on various spiritual allies as well as themselves. Many believe in divine intervention, interactions between this world and the next, miracles, and the efficacy of prayer. These beliefs affect their actions. Have you read other books in which forms of magical realism are incorporated?

5. Tension between outsiders and insiders is an important theme in *The Secrets of the Plumed Saint.* Which characters transform from outsider to insider and vice versa? Have you experienced similar situations?

6. Several characters act in ways that present unexpected behaviors. For example, Doña Amargarita does not behave according to the stereotype of a passive, Hispanic female. She is abrasive. Her nickname, Amarga, means bitter, and she enjoys her power and position. Can you think of other characters who play against type?

7. Roman Catholic beliefs and rituals provide the backdrop and give a rhythm to life in Villa Vieja. Are these practices presented in a positive, balanced, or negative way – whether or not you share them? Explain.

8. In the United States, the period of 1960-1980 brought dramatic societal changes and the rise of political activism. How did these changes affect the lives of Hispanos and other "under-represented groups," especially in rural areas?

9. Which female characters' qualities do you admire?

10. Both oral and written traditions play crucial roles as a means of transmitting family and cultural history in *The Secrets of the Plumed Saint.* How are family stories passed on in your family? Do any aspects of the story bring up memories for you?

11. Jesse is both insider and outsider. How does his past shape his character and his motives? In what way do his personal beliefs influence the outcome of the story? What do you consider Jesse's worst transgression?

12. Community solidarity of Villa Vieja supersedes both the rules of the legal system and the Church. At the end of *The Secrets of the Plumed Saint,* the people of Villa Vieja assume the role of a tribunal. They hear witnesses, vote as a jury, and arrive at a verdict. They mete out punishment in the form of reparation. Had Filomeno

died, do you think the village would join forces to protect Paco?

13.   A well-intentioned act results in embarrassment, scandal, pain, and possibly, death. How does intent influence our current justice system? In the balance between punishment and mercy, which weighs more heavily? Do you agree or disagree with the villagers' decision?

14.   The characters undergo transformations, large and small. Which characters' changes affected you the most? Can you explain why?

15.   When the statue disappears from the chapel tensions between the villagers and the formal Church intensify. Once the mystery is solved, is there any evidence that the tensions between the two entities increased or lessened?

About the Author

Photograph by Peggy Herrington

Elizabeth Ann Galligan, Ph.D., poet and educator, retired in 2007 from Eastern New Mexico University and dared to write a novel. She enjoys the multicultural heritage of the Southwest and is enchanted by its ever-changing landscape. Her writing is informed by many years of teaching English to speakers of other languages in Brazil, Japan, on the Diné reservation, at Rikers Island jail, and in adult ESL programs in New York and California. The author admires the Hispanic and native cultures and religions of the Southwest. She was Coordinator of the Writing Lab at New Mexico Highlands University and has taught graduate courses in English as a Second Language, Bilingual Education, and Multicultural Education. She holds degrees in anthropology, Latin American Studies, and Curriculum and Instruction in Multicultural Teacher Education.

Galligan's poetry appears in several anthologies and journals and in a number of university publications. She created two chapbooks, *Poems at 65* and *Striations*. In 1990 she was honored with an Encouragement Award for Japanese haiku in English in the Itoën Tea Company contest. Other publications include academic articles and presentations. She authored a two-part series on artist Masami Teraoka in *The Japan Times, Tokyo*, English edition, and co-authored a six-part series on successful Japanese in New York. Her article, "Impressions of Kyoto," appeared in *N. Y. Journal Japan*. She helped edit and is a contributor to *Pioneers of Education: Essays in Honor of Paulo Freire* (Nova Press, 2007) and authored a chapter in the graduate literacy text entitled *Historical, Theoretical, and Sociological Foundations of Reading in the United States*, Boston, MA (Pearson, 2011).

The author lives in her city of choice, Albuquerque, New Mexico, where she pursues reading, writing, poetry, photography, and gazing at the Sandia Mountains. She is active in SouthWest Writers and Fixed & Free Poets and promotes poetry readings at local libraries. She served on the Portales Cultural Affairs Committee and the Planning Committee for the Bosque Redondo Memorial. The author is a member of the board of the Albuquerque Martin Luther King, Jr. Multicultural Council. *Secrets of the Plumed Saint* is her first novel.

CPSIA information can be obtained at www.ICGtesting.com
Printed in the USA
LVOW100830020512

279983LV00003BA/4/P